303362342 2

D1827324

Clare Connelly was raised in small-town Australia among a family of avid readers. She spent much of her childhood up a tree, Mills & Boon book in hand. Clare is married to her own real-life hero, and they live in a bungalow near the sea with their two children. She is frequently found staring into space—a surefire sign that she's in the world of her characters. She has a penchant for French food and ice-cold champagne, and Mills & Boon novels continue to be her favourite ever books. Writing for Modern is a long-held dream. Clare can be contacted via clareconnelly.com or at her Facebook page.

VOWS ON THE VIRGIN'S TERMS

CLARE CONNELLY

MILLS & BOON

First published in Great Britain 2021
by Mills & Boon, an imprint of HarperCollins*Publishers* Ltd,
1 London Bridge Street, London, SE1 9GF

www.harpercollins.co.uk

HarperCollins*Publishers*
1st Floor, Watermarque Building,
Ringsend Road, Dublin 4, Ireland

Large Print edition 2022

Vows on the Virgin's Terms © 2021 Clare Connelly

ISBN: 978-0-263-29513-9

04/22

MIX
Paper from
responsible sources
FSC™ C007454

This book is produced from independently certified
FSC™ paper to ensure responsible forest management.
For more information visit www.harpercollins.co.uk/green.

Printed and Bound in the UK using 100% Renewable
Electricity at CPI Group (UK) Ltd, Croydon, CR0 4YY

This is a book for every girl who's ever been told she's 'bossy', but really just knows what she wants in life and isn't afraid to reach out and grab it.

CHAPTER ONE

IF OLIVIA COULD have closed her eyes and disappeared to *anywhere* else in the world, then she absolutely would have done so. But, having tricked Luca Giovanardi's assistant into revealing that he would be attending this all-star event, spent money she could ill afford on a budget airfare to Italy, and actually turned up at the party on the banks of the Tiber, she knew she'd crossed the point of no return.

There was nothing for it.

Her eyes scanned the crowds, feasting on the unfamiliar elegance and sophistication, a churning in her gut reminding her, every second, that she didn't belong here. It was so removed from her normal life, so different from what she was used to.

The party was in full swing, the restaurant courtyard packed with affluent guests, the fragrance in the air a heady mix of night-flowering jasmine and cloying floral perfume. As she studied the swarming crowd of glitterati, a woman bustled past, bumping Olivia, so she offered a tight smile of apology automatically, despite having done nothing worse than stand like a statue, frozen to the spot, too afraid to move deeper into the crowd, despite the fact she'd come here for exactly this purpose.

Naturally, he was in the centre.

Not just of the party, but of a group of people—men and women—his obvious charisma keeping each in his thrall, so that as he spoke their eyes were glued to his chiselled symmetrical face.

Why did he have to be so handsome? This wouldn't be so difficult if he were ordinary looking. Or even just an ordinary man. But everything about Luca Giovanardi was quite famously extraordinary, from his family's fall from grace to his spectacular resurrection to the top of the world's financial elite. As for his personal life, Olivia had gleaned only what was absolutely necessary from the Internet—but it had been enough to know that he was the polar opposite of her in every way. Where she was a twenty-four-year-old virgin who'd never even been so much as *kissed* by a man before, Luca was every inch the red-blooded male, a bachelor ever since his brief, long-ago marriage ended, a bachelor who made no attempt to conceal the speed with which he churned through glamorous, sexy women.

Was she really aiming to be one of them?

Olivia licked her lips, her throat suddenly parched, and, despite the fact she was alone, she shook her head, needing to physically push the idea from her mind. She wasn't aiming to become his mistress; what she needed was to become his wife.

A drum seemed to beat inside her body, gentle at first, the same drum beat she'd been hearing for years, since she'd first learned of her father's will and the implications contained therein for her, and her life. But now, as she stared at Luca, the drum was growing louder, more intense, filling her body with a tempo that was both unnerving and compelling.

There must have been two hundred people, at least, in the courtyard, and yet, at the very moment she moved a single foot, with the intention of cutting a path through the crowd and getting his attention, his eyes lifted and speared hers, the directness of his stare forcing her lips apart as a shot of breath fired from her body, the searing heat of his appraising glance the last thing she'd expected. So much for making her way to him! Her legs were filled with cement suddenly, completely immovable.

She'd seen photographs of him—there were no shortage of images online—but they hadn't prepared her for the real, three-dimensional image of Luca, and the way his nearness would affect her. His eyes were dark—like the bark of the old elm that grew at the rear of Hughenwood House. But not in summer, so much as winter, after a heavy rain, when it glistened and shimmered. A tremble ran the length of her spine. Olivia blinked away, needing relief. But even as her eyes landed on the moonlit river that snaked through this ancient city, she could feel his eyes on her, warming her flesh, tracing the lines of her face and body in a way she'd never known before.

Almost as if they had their own free will, her eyes dragged back towards him, skating over the other guests, hoping to find someone—something—that would serve as a life raft. But there was nothing that could compare to the magnetism of Luca Giovanardi—and Olivia was sunk.

When her eyes met his, he smirked, as if to say 'knew you couldn't resist me', and then he turned back to his companions, resuming whatever story had held them in his thrall all along.

Olivia's heart sank to her toes.

This wouldn't work if she found her husband attractive. She wanted a businesslike marriage, ordained purely to free up her inheritance. There was to be no personal connection between them, nothing that could make their marriage messier than it already was.

And yet, how could she *not* find him appealing? Despite evidence to the contrary—a spectacularly uninteresting love life—Olivia was still a woman, and she recognised a drop-dead gorgeous guy when he was paraded right beneath her nose. Who wouldn't recognise how damned hot Luca Giovanardi was? From his chiselled features, swarthy complexion, hair that was thick and dark and rough on top as though he made a habit of dragging his fingers through it, to a physique that was half wild animal and half man, all sinew and lean muscular strength, a figure that was barely contained by his obviously bespoke suit. It fitted him like a glove physically, but his spirit was too primal for such elegant tailoring. He should be naked. The thought had her sitting up straighter, mouth dry, and before she could help herself an image of him *sans* clothes exploded into her mind— the details undoubtedly inaccurate for lack of personal experience with anything approaching a naked man, but it was still enough to bring colour to her pale cheeks.

One thing was certain: Luca was not the kind of man one simply propositioned out of nowhere. Even with the leverage she felt she'd found it was almost impossible to believe it would be enough. She was perfectly *au fait* with *her* reasons for needing this marriage, but why in the world would a man like Luca, who had the world eating out of the palm of his hands, accept what she was intending to suggest?

She forced her legs to move once more, but, rather than taking her towards Luca, they fed her away from the party, skirting the edges of it, until she arrived in a quiet spot near a table of empty glasses, with one solitary waiter sitting on an upturned milk crate, smoking a cigarette. Olivia pretended not to notice him as she made her way to the railing, curling her hands over it and staring down at the river, her stomach in a thousand knots.

Coward.

Are you really going to leave without even asking him?

Did you ever think you'd go through with this?

It wasn't as though she'd told Sienna or their mother, Angelica, what she'd planned, so they wouldn't hold the failure against her. Yet despite that, how could Olivia ever face them, knowing she had the power to fix their futures, and had simply balked at the first hurdle?

For the briefest moment, the threat of tears stung Olivia's azure eyes, but it had been a long time since she'd cried, let alone run the risk of anyone *seeing* her cry, so she bit down on her lower lip until the urge passed, focusing on blotting her emotions completely, so that, a moment later, she was able to straighten her spine and turn around, ready to return to the party and once more weigh up her options—or torment herself with the path she knew she had to take, even when she was terrified to do so.

The waiter had disappeared, leaving the up-ended crate and a lingering odour of second-hand smoke that made Olivia's nose wrinkle as she passed. She turned her head to avoid the aroma, and as a result of not looking in the direction she was walking, stepped right into a rock-hard wall of a human's chest.

'Oh!' She tore her face back, apologising before she could make sense of what had happened, so even before she realised that the strong hands curling around her forearms to steady her belonged to Luca Giovanardi, she heard herself say, 'I'm so sorry, I didn't see you.'

'Now, we both know that is a lie,' he responded, his voice deep and gruff, and so much more sensual than she had ever known a voice could be. Her heart went into overdrive as she was confronted with, in many ways, her very worst nightmare.

Olivia sprang back from him, needing space urgently. She looked around, wishing now that the waiter were in evidence.

'Are you leaving?' Her question blurted out. His answering response, a slow-spreading grin, was like being bathed in warm caramel. Olivia tried not to feel the effects of it, but how could she resist? Nothing in her life had prepared her for this.

'No.'

'Oh.' Her relief was purely because that meant she hadn't lost her opportunity to do this. 'Good.'

When his eyes met hers, the speculation in them was unmistakable. Oh, God. This was going from bad to worse. It was bad enough that she had imagined him naked, but that he might feel a similar curiosity about her...

'I take it you are not leaving, either?'

'I—no. Why?'

'This is the exit.' He nodded towards the garden.

'Oh.' She furrowed her brow. 'I didn't—no. I just needed space.'

He lifted a brow. 'And now, *bella*? Have you had enough space?'

Bella? Beautiful? A shudder ran through her. She was *not* beautiful. At least, she desperately didn't want to be. Not in the way any man might notice and praise her for. She was not going to be like her mother—praised for her looks, adored for them, and then resented for them and the power they wielded. It was one of the reasons she'd refused to dress up tonight, choosing to wear a pair of simple black pants and a cream linen blouse—nothing that could draw attention to her figure, nothing that could draw attention to *her* at all.

'Olivia,' she supplied quickly, stopping herself from revealing her surname by clamping her lips together.

'Luca.' He held out a hand, as if to shake hers, but when Olivia placed hers in Luca's grip, he lifted it to his lips, placing a delicate kiss across her knuckles. Delicate it might have been, but the effect of her central nervous system was cataclysmic. She jerked her hand away, her blood pressure surely reaching dangerous levels now.

'I know.' Her own voice was croaky; she cleared it. Don't be such a coward! Get this over with. 'Actually…' She dug her fingernails into her palms. 'You're the reason I'm here tonight.'

His expression didn't change, yet she was aware of a tightening in his frame, a tension radiating from him now that hadn't been there a moment ago.

'Am I?' There was dark scepticism in his words, and she wondered at that. 'And why is that?'

'I came to speak to you.'

'I see.'

Was that disappointment in the depths of his eyes? She'd been wrong before. They were nothing like bark. Nothing so ordinary. These were eyes that were as dark as the sky, as determined as iron, as fascinating as every book ever written. She was losing herself in their intricacies, committing each spec to memory when she should have been focusing on what she needed to say!

'Well?' he drawled, and now his cynicism was unmistakable. 'What would you like to discuss?'

Her heart stammered. *Say it.* But how in the world could Olivia Thornton-Rose stand there and propose marriage to Luca Giovanardi? It was so ridiculous that, out of nowhere, she laughed, a tremulous, eerie sound, underscored by a lifting of her fingers to her forehead. She ran them across her brow, searching for words.

'There are two reasons women generally approach me,' he said quietly. 'Either with an investment "opportunity"...' he formed air quote marks around the word '...or to suggest a more...personal arrangement. Why don't you say which it is you have come to discuss?'

She sucked in a jagged breath, his arrogance wholly unexpected. But somehow, it made things easier, because he reminded her, ever so slightly, of her father in that moment, and that in turn made her feel just a little bit of hate for him—a hate that helped her face the necessity of what she'd come to do.

'I suppose, if we have to place this conversation into one of those two categories, it would certainly be the former, and not the latter.'

His eyes probed hers for longer than was necessary, then swept down to her lips, blazing a line of fire and heat as he went. 'Shame,' he murmured. 'I am not interested in any further business opportunities at present. However, a personal connection would have been quite satisfying to explore.'

Her stomach rolled and tumbled and her breath seemed to burn inside her lungs, making breathing almost impossible. Stars danced behind her eyelids. 'Impossible,' she managed to squeak out, wishing for her trademark cool in that moment. 'I'm not interested in that, at all.'

His features showed that he knew that to be a lie. Was she so obvious? Of course she was. She had no experience. How could she conceal what she was feeling from someone like Luca? She was a lamb to slaughter.

'Then I cannot see what we have to discuss.'

Do it. Get it over with. What's the worst that can happen? That he'll say no?

'I know about the bank you're trying to buy.'

He straightened, regarding her with a new level of interest. She'd surprised him, the words the last thing he'd expected to hear from her.

'Everyone knows about the offer I have made,' he hedged with admirable restraint, as though it were no big deal.

'Yes.' She offered a small smile, trying to defuse the tension that was pulling between them, and failing miserably. 'Of course, it's not a secret.'

He didn't say anything in response, and his silence seemed to stretch between them.

'You want to buy a bank, one of the oldest in Europe, and the board won't sell because of your playboy reputation. They're conservative and you're...not.'

His features—briefly—glowered before he resumed an expression of non-concern. His control was impressive.

'In addition, your father—'

'My father is none of your business,' he bit out crisply, surprising her with his vehemence. So those wounds still smarted, then? Despite the passage of twelve years, it seemed Luca hadn't recovered from the scandal that befell his father—his whole family—and the part he'd played in it.

'Actually, that's not exactly true.'

Luca's eyes narrowed. 'Ah. I see. Is this another debt of his? Money owed from him to you?' He frowned. 'But you are too young, so perhaps it is a debt to someone else, someone you love?'

Olivia's heart thumped. Someone she loved? Was there any such person? Sienna, of course, she thought of her younger sister with an ache in the region of her heart. But beyond Sienna, Olivia was alone in the world. There was no one else she loved. Her mother, she pitied, and felt a great deal of duty to care for, but loved? It was far too complicated to be described in that way, and impossible to express in such simplistic terms.

'It's not like that.'

Luca's nostrils flared. 'Then why do you not get to the point and tell me what it *is*, rather than what it is not?'

'I'm trying,' she promised from between clenched lips. 'But you're kind of intimidating, you know?'

Her honesty had surprised him. He took a step backwards, tilted his face away, drew in a deep enough breath to make his chest shift visibly, then expelled it slowly, before turning back to face her.

'I cannot help being who I am.'

'I know. But, just—bear with me. This isn't easy.'

He crossed his arms over his chest—hardly painting a picture of calm acceptance. She bit down on her lower lip then stopped when his eyes dropped to the gesture.

'Perhaps we should start with my father, not yours. I imagine you've heard of him. Thomas Thornton-Rose?'

Luca's demeanour shifted, his features changing, as he disappeared back in time. 'He was a friend to my father. During the trial, he supported him. There were not many who did.'

'They were very close friends,' Olivia agreed with a murmur, wondering then if he knew about the will. There was no recognition in his features beyond that which was perfectly appropriate to an acquaintance of his father.

'He passed away shortly after my father went to prison. I remember reading a headline.'

'Yes.' Olivia blinked quickly, focusing on the Castel Sant'Angelo, a short distance away, glowing gold against the inky sky. 'It was very sudden.' Her brows knitted together. 'He hadn't been ill or anything. None of us expected—' She swallowed, ignoring the lump in her throat.

'I'm sorry.'

She brushed aside his condolences. 'That's not necessary.'

Her cool response had him arching a thick, dark brow. Olivia didn't notice.

'Shortly after he died, the terms of his will came to light. You would know that we're part of the British aristocracy, with much land and money held up in various investments?'

He lifted his shoulders in an indolent shrug. 'I do not know much more than we have already discussed. Should I?'

Another maniacal laugh erupted from her chest. He didn't know anything about this, and he didn't know anything about her? Panic was swallowing her whole. She'd counted on a degree of insight, but that had been foolish. After all, his father had been in prison a long time. She doubted they had regular tête-à-tête regarding their lives.

She would need to start from scratch. Careful to keep the anxiety from her voice, she began slowly. 'When my father died, it was discovered that his estate was carved up in a particularly unusual—' *cruel*, she mentally substituted '—way. My mother was to inherit nothing, and my sister and I would only inherit if we met very specific circumstances, by the time we turn twenty-five.'

His features gave nothing away. 'And what circumstances are these?'

Do it. Stop freaking out. He'll say no, and you

can go home again. And do what? Kick your mother out of the family home? Hand the keys over to horrid second cousin, Timothy?

'Well, it's very clear. You see, my father was very...' she searched for a word that was more socially acceptable than 'misogynistic' '...old-fashioned.'

He dipped his head forward. 'And this is a problem?'

She ignored his interjection. He'd understand, soon enough.

'He never believed women to be capable of managing their own financial affairs.' She couldn't look at Luca as she spoke, and so didn't see the expression of disgust that briefly marred his handsome features. And with good reason— since rebuilding his family empire, Luca had prided himself on employing a diverse work-force. His executive team was made up of more women than men. It had never occurred to him to discriminate based on gender.

'When my parents married, my mother signed over her life savings to him—she'd been an actress, quite successful here in Italy, and had earned well. But she was very young—only just twenty, whereas he was nineteen years older. She loved him.' Olivia's voice curled with a hint of disdain at the very idea of love, and Luca, who was an expert in nuance, responded to the subtle inflection by leaning infinitesimally closer. 'She trusted him.' It was impossible to flatten the emotion from her tone, but she didn't convey the depths of her anger—how her father had abused that trust, because young Angelica had made one mistake, had a silly youthful indiscretion, and for that she'd been punished every day for the rest of her life, no matter how hard she tried to fix things, no matter how often she apologised. Olivia turned to face him, her clear, blue eyes spiking through his black. 'My father managed everything, so that when he died, she had no idea how their affairs were arranged. She couldn't have known that he'd manipulated the estate to curtail everything away from her.'

'What reason could your father have had for doing this?'

His incredulity touched something in the pit of her stomach.

'He was angry with her,' she mouthed, clearing her throat, the barbarism of her father's final act something that had stung her for years. Olivia waved a hand through the air. 'It was ancient history by the time he died, a silly mistake my mother made, many years earlier. Clearly nothing can justify his decision.'

Luca compressed his lips, and her eyes fell to them, so something white hot radiated from low down in her abdomen, spreading through her body with fierce urgency, stealing her breath and weakening her knees. She wrenched her gaze away, unable to make sense of the emotions that were rioting through her. The truth was, the unmistakable rush of desire she felt for him made her want to turn tail and run, to hide from the things she was experiencing. Olivia considered herself to be an expert at hiding her feelings, but she was also used to her feelings making much more sense.

'He was never going to leave any part of the family fortune to our mother, nor to me and Sienna.'

'Nothing about that makes sense. Does he have other children? From an earlier relationship?'

'No.' An anguished smile tormented her beautiful face. 'If only it were that simple. There's only us. And in order to know that the money would be in safe hands, he had his will drafted to specify that Sienna and I must marry, by our twenty-fifth birthdays. Only then will our portion of inheritance become legally ours. Only then could he trust "his money" would be in safe hands.'

'And your mother?'

'She was granted a very small stipend. But it's been lessening every year and stops completely when we turn twenty-five. My birthday is next month.'

She caught the coarse swear word he issued from between clenched teeth. 'With respect, your father sounds like a jackass.'

Her eyes flew wide, and amusement bubbled through her. Were the situation not so very dire, she might have given into it and laughed, or even leaned forward and pressed her hand to his chest, to share the moment of agreement, but worry still dragged at her every breath.

'He was…very set in his ways,' she said, puzzling at the deep sense of loyalty that still ran through her. Even after all he'd done, after the nightmare he'd made all their lives, she felt driven to defend him.

Luca made a sound that suggested her description barely scratched the surface.

'I wouldn't be here if I weren't completely desperate.' Her voice snagged a little and she angled her face away, wondering why she was finding it so difficult to hold onto her usual reserve. 'When my father died, I was only twelve. I had no control of our finances, no insight into what my mother was spending. She continued to rack up enormous debts, maxing out all the credit cards she had, as well as a hefty line of credit set against the house. By the time I was old enough to see what was going on, things were dire. I have tried, Luca. I have tried to fix things, but there is never enough money to make even a dint in the debt. I have to work jobs close to home, and that limits my options, plus I'm not qualified for anything.' She shook her head, surprised at how much she was confessing to him. It was as though, having started, she couldn't put a lid on her feelings.

Drawing in a deep breath, Olivia tried again. 'We have lived on the breadline for years. I have scrimped and saved and done everything I can to get by, but it's no use. If it were just me, I would walk out of Hughenwood House and never look back. But I can't leave my mother saddled with hundreds of thousands of pounds in debt. I can't let my father do this to Mum and Sienna.' Not on top of everything else he'd already done. 'I won't let him do this to us.' The words were laced with a quiet, determined vehemence, but it was clear that they came from the very depths of her being.

'As I said, your father sounds like a jackass.' A hint of sympathy softened the words, surprising her and bringing an ache to her throat. 'But I cannot see why you have sought me out to tell me all this, unless you think my father has some control over the will?' He scanned her face, and she had the strangest sensation he was pulling her apart, piece by piece. 'If that is the case, I must disappoint you. I have no sway with my father. You would be better to approach him directly, believe me.'

'No, no, that's not it.' She fluttered a hand through the air then brought it to the bridge of her nose, pinching it between forefinger and thumb. 'If I don't get married soon, per the will, then the inheritance defaults to my second cousin. It's not just the money, but our *home*. Our family home.' To Olivia's chagrin, her voice cracked, and she tilted her chin defiantly, angered by the weak emotional display, and even more so by the fact the house still meant so much to her, despite the unhappiness they'd experienced within its walls. 'It's the only home my mother has, and it would kill her to have to leave.'

He crossed his arms over his chest. 'I'm not a matchmaker, *cara*. Besides, I find it hard to believe you would have any difficulty finding a man willing to play the part of your groom.'

As he offered the compliment, his eyes slid lower, to the outline of her breasts, barely revealed by the boxy linen shirt she wore. Despite that, heat simmered in her veins and, to her shame, her nipples puckered against the fabric of her bra, straining—but for what? Her eyes flew to his hands and she knew what she wanted, needed. For him to touch her. Intimately. All over.

She swallowed a groan and looked away, using every ounce of her determination to maintain a frigid expression.

'It cannot be *any* man.' Her voice took on a wooden quality. 'My father was explicit about that too.'

Silence hummed and crackled between them, anticipation stretching her nerves to breaking point. Did he know what was coming? She risked a glance at him but was none the wiser; she couldn't read what he was thinking.

'I have to marry *you*, Luca. No one else. You.'

CHAPTER TWO

IT WAS OBVIOUS just by looking at Luca that he was a man who prized his control and strength, but in that moment Olivia could have blown him over with a feather. It was, quite clearly, the last thing he'd expected her to say.

'You're saying—'

'That I need to marry you,' she confirmed, forcing herself to meet his eyes even when something sparked between them that set her blood racing at a million miles an hour. 'And that marrying me could be very good for you, too.'

'This makes no sense.'

'I know.' She bit down on her lip. 'I was really hoping you'd know about this whole thing.'

'My father and I are not exactly on speaking terms.'

She pulled a face, sympathy flooding her. But then, she knew more than enough about difficult family relationships.

'But they made the agreement so long ago. I just presumed, over the years…'

'It was never discussed with me.'

'Me either,' she promised. 'The first I heard about it was when the solicitors appeared at Hughenwood, grim-faced and stern.'

'How did you learn about the bank I am buying?'

'Trying to buy,' she corrected valiantly, because his desire to acquire the bank, and their determined rebuffing of his offers, was at the heart of her inducement. 'I read about it online. Why?'

'So you researched me, prior to coming here tonight?'

'Given that I came here intending to propose marriage to a man I'd never met, naturally I did some preparation.'

A curl of derision shifted the shape of his mouth. 'Then perhaps you also read that I have already been married once. It was, in every way, an unmitigated disaster. I have no intention of ever—' he leaned closer, so close that if she pushed up onto the tips of her toes, she could kiss him '—marrying again. *Capisce?*'

'This wouldn't be a normal marriage,' she said quietly, glad that years of living in the war zone that was her parents' relationship had left her with nerves of steel—or the appearance of them, at least. 'I don't want a husband any more than you want a wife.'

'I'm sorry, I thought you just asked me to marry you?'

'Yes,' she responded quickly. 'For the sake of satisfying a clause in my father's will. But our marriage would be a sham—nothing more than our names on a piece of paper.'

He stared down at her, his features inscrutable, so she had no idea what he was thinking. With a sense she was losing her argument, she clutched for the only straw she held in her possession. 'My family's name is well respected. Marriage to anyone would increase your chances with the bank's uber conservative board—but marriage to a Thornton-Rose, in particular, would improve your standing.' She had made her peace with this offer many weeks ago, but as she said it now, as she heard herself actually trading on her father's hated, hated surname, she wanted the world to open up and swallow her whole.

But freedom would be worth it. If she could just get him to agree, the money would be hers and she could finally fix everything her father broke—her mother would finally have some security and stability. And, most importantly, Olivia's beloved younger sister Sienna would be saved from having to make her own arcane match to inherit any part of the fortune—they simply wouldn't need the money.

'And you are suggesting I could use your ancient name to curry favour with a group of prejudiced snobs? That this is how I operate in business?' His sneer of derision warmed her to the centre of her being. She couldn't have said why, but his immediate rejection of that idea was a relief. 'I do not need your father's name to succeed, *bella*, just as I have never needed my own father's name.'

Admiration expanded inside her. He was right—everything he'd achieved had been off his own back. And yet, from what she'd read online, he wanted the bank more than anything else—and she was sure their marriage would help him achieve it. She narrowed her gaze, focusing on that salient detail. 'You want to buy the Azzuri Bank, and I believe our marriage would make that easier.'

'I don't do things the easy way.'

Her heart skipped a beat and she realised, all at once, that this wasn't going to be enough. She didn't hold enough of an incentive for Luca to agree to this. Why had she even allowed herself a glimmer of hope?

'Well, that's a lovely privilege to have.'

'Privilege,' he repeated with disbelief.

'Oh, yes, privilege.' She turned away from him, stalking back to the railing and staring out at the river. It had seen so much over the millennia, so many tragedies and heartbreaks, so much joy and delight. Her own emotions spilled towards it, adding to the multitude of experience. 'What must it be like to be able to turn down offers of help?'

'You said it yourself, you come from a very wealthy family. Do you really think you have any right to complain to me about privilege?'

'Wealthy, in theory, yes,' she responded, turning to look at him over her shoulder, only to realise he'd moved to stand right beside her and was staring at her in a way that made her feel as though she was completely naked—not in a physical sense, but right down to her soul. 'But not privileged. And not free. Do you have any idea—?' She bit back the words, shaking her head.

'Finish what you were going to say.'

'Why? There's no point, is there?' Her shimmering blue eyes caught his, scanning them, hunting them for answers. 'You've already made your decision.'

'My first decision, yes,' he agreed. 'I want no part of any marriage.' Was she imagining the slight hesitation to his voice? Yes. Of course she was. Men like Luca Giovanardi didn't hesitate about anything.

'Then I'll go,' she whispered, accepting her fate, numb to the future that lay before her.

'Not before you have explained some more,' he insisted, with a firmness to his tone that made it almost impossible to argue.

But Olivia was used to being dictated to, and had learned how to harden herself to another's commands. 'Is there any point if you've made up your mind?'

'We won't know unless you try.'

Hope beat wings inside her chest, but she refused to let it carry her away. He was offering her a chance, but it was very slim. She searched for words yet her brain refused to cooperate. She groaned, turning back to the river.

'Start with this,' he suggested, the gentleness of his voice making her stomach churn. She hadn't expected anything like that, from him. 'How exactly did you imagine this marriage would work?'

It was something—a way in. But was he simply trying to make her understand how stupid the whole idea had been? She sucked in a deep breath and forced her nerves to slow down.

'Well.' She spoke slowly. 'I thought a businesslike agreement would be best for the both of us.'

His brows shot up. 'A businesslike marriage? Isn't that a contradiction in terms?'

'Not for people like you and me?'

'And what exactly are we like, *bella*?'

'Please, don't call me that. My name is Olivia.'

He nodded, brushing aside her request.

'Both fundamentally opposed to marriage.' She returned to her original train of thought. 'You don't want a wife, and I don't want a husband. Therefore, we can dictate the terms of our marriage, making sure they suit us completely.'

'And what terms would you suggest?'

Something like danger prickled along her skin. Desires she had no business feeling, let alone voicing, spliced her in half. She did everything she could to ignore them. After all, desire was at the root of her mother's downfall. Love. Allowing herself to be swept up in a man's promises, a man's charisma, blinding her to reality, had led to Olivia's mother's life of misery—Olivia never intended to be so foolish.

'That's the beauty of what I'm offering,' she said quietly, trying to pick up the threads of the speech she'd prepared on the flight over. 'This would be a marriage in name only. I'd live in England, you'd live in Italy, and when a suitable amount of time had passed, we would quietly, simply file for divorce. After our wedding day, we'd never have to see one another again.'

He studied her in a way that sent little barbs running through her body. His eyes seemed to see everything, to perceive everything, so years of practice hiding her emotion no longer seemed to serve her. She struggled to maintain a mask of composure in the face of his obvious interest.

'I can see you've thought this through, but you've miscalculated. The promise of your name is not enough to induce me into marriage, with you, or anyone.'

She swept her eyes shut, failure inevitable now. 'I see.'

'You said that if you don't inherit, your portion of the family fortune goes to a cousin. Do you know this person?'

She shuddered involuntarily. 'Yes.'

'Is he the kind of person who would act in self-interest, to secure this inheritance?'

She bit into her lower lip. 'He would only stand to inherit *if* you and I don't get married.'

'Or...' he let the word hang between them '...if he challenged the validity of our marriage.'

She blinked up at him. 'But—could he do that?'

'It is my experience that people are capable of all sorts of things, when large sums of money are involved.'

She crossed her arms over her chest, then immediately wished she hadn't when his eyes lowered to the swell of roundness there. Anticipation ran like little waves across her skin. 'So what do you suggest?'

'I do not intend to make a suggestion, Olivia. Only to point out that the neat and tidy marriage you've imagined would never have worked.'

Of course, he was right. She should have seen all the angles. They were talking about a multi-million-pound inheritance. If they were going to fake a marriage, it had to be plausible. 'Then, what if we were to marry—' she thought quickly '—and live together, here in Rome, but only as housemates. Separate bedrooms, separate lives.'

His lips curled with a hint of derision. 'I cannot see what is in that for me.'

'Azzuri Bank—'

'I will acquire the bank, Olivia, on my own terms. Of that, I have no doubt.'

A shiver ran the length of her spine. His determination was borderline ruthless—she didn't doubt he'd succeed, and now felt a degree of foolishness for ever thinking a man like Luca Giovanardi could be tempted by something as flimsy as having her as a wife.

'If you want to tempt me to agree to this, you must think of something to offer beyond the bank.' A test? He was staring at her as if weighting her reaction.

Her cheeks went from paper white to rosy pink within a second. 'Are you saying you would want our marriage to be—intimate? Because I have to tell you, I have no interest in becoming another notch on your very well-studded bedpost.'

A cynical smile changed his face completely. The smile whispered things into her soul. *Liar.* 'I'm not so desperate that I need to blackmail women into my bed.'

'No, of course not,' she dismissed quietly, wishing they were more like equals when it came to relationships. 'You probably have a line snaked around the block.'

His obsidian eyes narrowed. 'I was not referring to sex.'

'Then what did you mean?'

He scanned her face, and she wondered if he was going to dwell on the suggestion of a physical relationship. 'If we were to marry, there would be no advantage to either of us in maintaining separate lives, under the same roof. News of our marriage would inevitably break in the press, and then, public scrutiny would follow. A housekeeper could be bribed to provide details of our living arrangements. These things happen.'

'I hadn't thought of that,' she admitted.

'We would need to create the fiction of a passionate, whirlwind romance, for as long as it took to satisfy the terms of the will—I would imagine thirty days would be sufficient.' He lifted his shoulders in a charismatic, indolent shrug. 'To that end, we would need to share a bed.'

Her lips parted to form a perfect 'o'. How she wished she had more experience with men in that moment! 'Surely that's not necessary.'

'I have staff.'

'Couldn't they take a holiday for the duration of our marriage? A month isn't very long.' Except when you were sharing a bed with a man like this!

His lips twisted into a cynical smile. 'Don't worry, *cara*. I have no interest in sex becoming a part of our marriage. It would be purely for show.'

She stared at him, aghast. She wanted to demur, to fight him on this point, but something was shifting between them, and she no longer felt that failure was imminent. If anything, he was positioning himself to accept. She tilted her head, not quite a nod, but at least not a denial either.

'It is a big bed. You'll cope.'

She swallowed, her throat visibly knotting, then jerked her head once more, this time in agreement.

'Are you saying you'll agree to do this?'

He considered her for several long moments. Could he hear the rushing of her heart over the sound of the nearby party? Surely. It beat hard and fast, a fast-paced drum, hard against her ribs. He turned away from her abruptly, staring out at the river, his face in profile like something crafted from stone. She stared at him against her will, unable to draw her eyes away. He was captivating and magnetic, completely overpowering. It was not hard to understand how he had made such a success of himself and his life.

'There is something personal about me you would not have discovered on the Internet.'

She frowned, wondering at his tone, the darkness to his voice.

'My *nonna* is ill.'

The words were spoken quietly and yet they fell between them like rock boulders.

Olivia leaned closer, as if that might help her understand better.

'Not ill.' He turned to face her, the strength in his gaze sending a pulse radiating through her. 'She is dying.'

'I'm sorry to hear that.' Olivia's voice was gentle, sincere. 'Are you close?'

A grimace tightened his lips. 'Yes.' He paused, seeming to weigh his words. 'She has been my biggest support. I owe her a lot.'

'I'm sure she supported you out of love. Seeing you make such a success of yourself is undoubtedly all she wants from you.'

His smile showed a hint of affection. 'She is still an Italian *nonna*, and cannot help meddling. She has expressed, on many occasions, a desire for me to marry.' The words wrapped around Olivia, steadier than steel. 'She worries about me.'

'Worries about *you*?' Olivia couldn't help remarking, the very idea of this man being the object of anyone's concern almost laughable.

He didn't look at her, nor did he respond.

'If we were to create the impression of a passionate, whirlwind love affair, it might go some of the way to easing her concerns.'

Olivia's eyes flared wide. 'You want to lie to her?'

'We would be legally married,' he pointed out. 'That is not a lie.'

'But a love affair,' she said with a soft shake of her head. 'No one would believe it.'

His eyes narrowed as he stared at her. 'They must. This marriage must convince your cousin, your father's probate solicitors and my grandmother. It must convince the world.'

Something twisted inside her. Surprise. Hope. It wasn't exactly an agreement, but, for a moment, he sounded as though he was seriously contemplating this. She might actually be getting somewhere—and that knowledge both excited and terrified her.

'If your grandmother wants you to get married, why haven't you done so before now?'

'Marriage is not a mistake I intend to make twice. Even for her.'

'But we're discussing marriage now.'

'A very different kind of marriage,' he pointed out. 'One with clear-cut rules and boundaries. One that precludes, by design, any emotion whatsoever.'

'Are you saying you'll agree to this?'

He stared at her long and hard, so long, so hard, that any pretence she might have liked to maintain that she felt nothing for him flew out of her soul and swam away on the crest of the Tiber. It was all physical—surely she could control that?

'I would have conditions of my own.'

Her heart skipped a beat. 'I see. Such as?'

He turned to face her now, looking just as he had the first moment they'd met, but with a hint of grief still stirring in the depths of his eyes, so Olivia was forced to re-evaluate her appraisal of him as a cold, ruthless tycoon. He clearly had a heart, and a large part of it, she suspected, belonged to his *nonna*. 'My grandmother would need to believe this is real.' He pressed a thumb to his middle finger on the opposing hand, counting off a list. 'There would need to be discretion and respect. No affairs for either of us.'

'Easier for me than you, I suspect,' she said, before she could stop herself. After all, the man's prowess as a bachelor was a well-established fact.

He let the barb sail by.

'This would be a marriage of practicality,' he continued with firm indifference, tapping another finger, not taking his eyes off her face. 'You'd get what you want, and I'd get what I want.' For a moment, his gaze dropped to her lips. 'This would not be a genuine relationship. We would not become friends. We would not have sex.'

A shiver ran down her spine as images of that sprang to mind before she could stop them, and, for the first time in her life, Olivia experienced a headlong rush of desire.

She kept her expression neutral with great effort. 'I'm not interested in your friendship. Or in having sex with you.'

He didn't smile. He didn't nod. He simply stared at her as though she were a mathematical equation he could understand, if only he looked long and hard enough.

'And what about love?'

It jolted her straight. She shook her head fiercely. 'No.'

His dark eyes narrowed speculatively.

'Absolutely not,' she rushed to reassure him, suppressing a shudder of sheer panic. It wasn't him, but the idea of submitting herself to any man, as her mother had her father, that sent arrows of terror down her spine. She wanted independence—true independence—and this she wouldn't find by falling in love.

'I'm not kidding. I will not run the risk of you fantasising about a relationship with me. It is something I never risk when I sleep with a woman.'

'But we won't be sleeping together.'

'No, we'll be married. That has the potential to be far more dangerous. You might start to think—'

'Believe me, I won't. If it weren't for this damned will, I'd never, ever say those vows. And the happiest day of my life will be when the ink dries on our divorce. Okay?'

'I'm curious,' he said slowly, so close the words breathed across her temple and she caught a hint of his masculine cologne. Goosebumps lifted on her skin.

'You are a beautiful, young woman. What happened to make you so opposed to marriage?'

'You don't hold the monopoly on disastrous marriages.'

'You've been married before?'

'No—I—didn't mean mine. My parents—' She shook her head, cleared her thoughts, and focused a steady, steel-like gaze on him. 'I was born with a brain,' she said after a beat. 'I don't see any reason to tie myself to a man. At least, not for real.'

'And do you promise me you will not change your mind? At no point in our marriage will you want more than I am willing to offer today?'

She tilted her face to his. 'Are you accepting my proposal?'

'Can you assure me that we can keep this businesslike?' he said thoughtfully.

'Absolutely.'

He considered that for several moments, and Olivia's pulse went into overdrive. So much hung in the balance for her. There was so much this marriage would achieve—not least, providing for her mother, securing their family home, and protecting Sienna. And yet it would come at a great personal cost for Olivia. To give into her father's misogynistic, sexist demands from beyond the grave rushed her skin like a rash, and anger speared her, despite the fact she'd made her peace with the necessity of this long ago.

'Fine.' He nodded once. 'Then we will marry.'

A shiver ran down her spine, even when he was giving her everything she'd wanted. Even when his acceptance was the first step on her pathway towards liberation. She forced her mouth into a smile, made her eyes hold his even when sparks of electricity seemed to be flying from Luca towards her, superheating her veins.

'Excellent,' she murmured, even when she had the strangest sense, for no reason she could grasp, that she was stepping right off the deep end with no idea how to swim.

After his divorce, Luca Giovanardi had destroyed almost every single piece of evidence that he had ever been married. There had been catharsis in that. He was only young—a boy, in many ways—and so the act of throwing his wedding back into the ruins of the Coliseum had felt immeasurably important, as though he were reclaiming a piece of himself. He had destroyed every photograph they'd had printed, and wiped almost all of them from his digital storage. He hadn't wanted to remember Jayne.

He hadn't ever wanted to think of her again. Not of how much he'd loved her, nor how happy he'd thought they were. He didn't want to think about the way his world had come storming down around his ears and then she'd turned her back on him, leaving him for one of his most despised business rivals, a man who had swept in and triumphed as Luca's father's empire had come crumbling down around them.

Luca had learned two lessons that day—never to believe in the fantasy of love, and never to trust a woman.

So what the hell had he just agreed to?

He gripped his glass of whisky, eyes focused straight ahead, without seeing the view. Olivia Thornton-Rose filled his mind. *'I wouldn't be here if I weren't completely desperate.'*

Besides, there was no danger here. No risk. This was nothing like the emotional suicide he'd committed the day he'd agreed to share his life with Jayne. This was sensible. Safe. And short-term.

More importantly, it met both their needs. For months, he'd been wishing he could do something to calm his grandmother, to ease her as she approached the end of her life. Her repeated entreaties for him to find that 'one someone special', to 'give love another chance', were offered kindly from her vantage point of having had a long and very happy marriage, but marriage was not even remotely on Luca's to-do list.

Until now.

He reached for his phone and dialled his grandmother's number before he could change his mind. 'Nonna?' He took a drink of Macallan. 'There's something I want to tell you.'

CHAPTER THREE

IT WAS LIKE being in a dream, a dream from which she couldn't wake. But wasn't it better than the nightmare that had been life before this? At least some relief was on the horizon.

It had, however, been a mistake not to see him again before the ceremony itself. A mistake not to inure herself a little to the sight of Luca Giovanardi, dressed to the nines, in a black tuxedo with a grey tie, shiny black shoes, and hair slicked back from his face. She stood beside him in the unbelievably extravagant dress she'd been talked into buying at Harrods, after Luca's assistant had called to explain that he'd organised an appointment with the bridal team there. She was aware of his every breath, the husky tone to his voice, the magnetism of the man, and felt as if she wanted to turn tail and bolt for the door.

A wedding 'in name only' had seemed like a simple idea at the time, but, now that they'd come to the actual commitment, the reality of what they were doing bore down on her like a ton of cement. She glanced across at Luca, his sombre profile making her breath snatch in her throat, so she looked away again, panic drumming through her. She wished, more than anything, for Sienna to be with her. It would have meant the world to be able to reach out and hold her sister's hand, to see her smiling, kind eyes and know that this wasn't sheer madness. Only Sienna would *never* have approved. She wouldn't have smiled from the sidelines as Olivia committed herself to this farce—she'd have fought tooth and nail to get her to stop. Even if that meant losing their house. Even if that meant letting their father punish their mother one last, cruel, lasting time.

The priest said something, and Luca turned to face Olivia, dragging her back to this moment, in which it was just the two of them, and the lie they were weaving. He spoke his vows first, in English in deference to her, before slipping an enormous diamond ring onto her finger. The simple contact sent a thousand little lightning bolts through her; standing was almost impossible.

When it was Olivia's turn to say the vows, the

priest spoke slowly, his accent thick, and Olivia stumbled on a few words. Nerves were playing havoc with her focus. She offered the priest an apologetic glance, before retrieving a simple gold band and pressing it to Luca's finger. Just like before, when he'd placed her ring on her finger, Olivia felt as though a marching band had started to run rampant through her veins. She pulled her hand away quickly, as though she'd been electrocuted, her eyes sliding to Luca's *nonna* without her intent. The happiness there was blatantly obvious—she had obviously bought the lie, hook, line and sinker. Olivia looked away again immediately, right into Luca's enormous dark eyes, their watchful intensity making her heart thunder.

'And that is it,' the priest said with a clap that completely undid the sombre nature of the ceremony. 'You may now kiss your bride.' He gestured to Olivia, and Olivia's heart seemed to grind to a halt. Oh, crap. How had she forgotten about this part?

Was it too late to back out? She stared at the priest with a sinking feeling, aware of Luca's *nonna*'s watchful gaze, then looked back up at the man who was now her husband.

Oh, God, oh, God, oh, God.

In name only. Except for right now.

Luca moved closer, one hand coming to rest on her hip, the other capturing her cheek, holding her face steady. His thumb padded over the flesh just beside her lip, low on her cheek, and goosebumps spread over her arms.

She wanted to tell him she couldn't do this, that she'd never even been kissed before, that too many people were watching, that she had no idea what she was doing, but then he was dropping his head, his mouth seeking hers as though it were the most natural thing in the world, and all she could do was surrender to the necessity of this. And the wonder.

Luca swore internally. His body had ignited, a flame of passion bursting through him the second their lips met. What had started as a perfunctory ceremonial requirement had blown way out of his control the second her lips parted beneath his and she made that husky little moan, pushing the sound deep into his throat. Screw ceremony. The hand that was on her hip slid around to her back, drawing her body hard against his, angling her slightly for privacy from his grandmother—not that he was capable of that degree of rational thought. Instincts had taken over completely. His mouth moved, deepening the kiss, his tongue flicking hers, and with every soft little moan she made he felt his control snapping, so within seconds he was fantasising about stripping the damned dress away and making love to her—not slowly and languidly, either, but hard and fast, as this passion bursting between them demanded.

Hell. This was a nightmare.

They had a deal, and at no point was he supposed to be attracted to his wife, of all people. At no point were they supposed to want each other like this. He wouldn't let this happen. Any other woman, fine. But not with his bride.

He wrenched his mouth from hers, and Olivia had to bite down on her lower lip to stop from crying out at the sudden withdrawal. Her eyes were heavy, drugged by desire, so that it took several seconds before she remembered where they were, and who they were surrounded by.

Mortification doused her sensual need. It had only been a kiss—albeit a passionate one—but in Olivia's innocent mind, they'd just done the first act of a live porno for Luca's grandmother and priest.

He was watching her in that intense way of

his, eyes hooded and unreadable, his own face notably *normal*, not flushed and passion-filled, as she was sure hers must be. Of *course* he looked like normal. This was Luca Giovanardi. The man literally went through women as most men did underwear. Or bottles of milk, at least. She stifled a moan and blanked her face of emotions—but too late, she feared. He must have seen how affected she was by the kiss. He must know how completely he took her breath away. How *easily*.

She sucked in a deep breath, and another. *It's okay. It's over now. You never need to kiss him or touch him ever again.* The thought was supposed to be reassuring, but her heart did a strange, twisty reaction, painful and impossible to ignore.

The next moment, his hand reached down and linked with hers, fingers intertwined, so she jerked her gaze back to his face. He smiled at her, but the smile got nowhere near his eyes.

'Come and meet my grandmother. *Cara.*' He added the term of endearment as an afterthought. It brought a rush of warmth to her. She ignored it. This was all for show, for his grandmother's benefit. That was part of their deal, and, given what he was sacrificing for her, he deserved her to play along to the best of her ability.

'Yes, of course.' Her voice sounded, blessedly, normal.

Pietra Giovanardi was past her eightieth birthday but she stood straight and proud, silver hair pulled over one shoulder, slender body wrapped in couture and diamonds, yet somehow she managed to look approachable and down to earth. Her lips were quick to smile, her face well lined by time, by life, and her eyes sparkled as the couple approached. There was no hint of the terminal illness Luca had mentioned, beyond a body that was painfully slim.

'Ahh, Luca, Luca, Luca, this is the happiest day of *my* life,' she exclaimed, lifting a shaking hand and patting her grandson's cheek affectionately, tears dampening her eyes as she turned to look at Olivia. She smiled brightly, emulating a happy bride. That was, after all, their deal.

'Signora Giovanardi,' Olivia murmured, but the older woman batted a hand through the air then drew Olivia into a warm hug, enveloping her in a softly floral fragrance at the same time she dislodged her hand from Luca's, leaving a cool feeling of absence that Olivia wished she hadn't noticed. The older woman was painfully thin, her bones barely covered by fine, papery skin. Sympathy spread like wildfire through Olivia at this obvious indication of her illness.

'You must call me Pietra,' she insisted. 'Or Nonna.'

'Pietra,' Olivia rushed, softening her haste with a softer smile. 'It's a pleasure to meet you.'

'Ah, no, the pleasure is mine. I thought this would never happen, after...' Pietra's voice briefly stalled but she covered quickly, moving on. She hadn't needed to finish anyway; Olivia knew what the older woman had been going to say. After his first marriage. For the first time since they'd agreed to this sham, she wondered about his past, his ex, and why the marriage had left him so badly scarred. But Nonna was moving on, steering the conversation forward. 'And here he's been keeping you a secret all this time.' Pietra made a tsking sound. 'But it is no business of mine. I won't ask the details. I'm just glad it has come to this. Now, shall we have some Prosecco?'

Olivia blinked up at Luca, expecting him to demur—the sooner they concluded their 'wedding', the sooner they could be free of the need to act like a pair of besotted newly-weds, and the sooner their thirty days of captivity could start.

'*Sì*, I have arranged it.'

Olivia's eyes widened, but she couldn't argue with him, obviously.

'You would be welcome to stay at Villa Tramonto tonight, as well,' Pietra offered as they walked from the church.

'My grandmother's villa,' Luca explained to Olivia. 'Nestled above Positano. You would love it, *cara*.' He was so good at this! With effortless ease, he made it seem as though they shared a genuine connection. His voice was soft, romantic, so her skin pricked with goosebumps she was sure his dark eyes observed, before he turned to Pietra. 'Another time. It is our wedding night, after all.'

Heat bloomed inside Olivia at the implication of his words—at how they would be spending tonight if they were anything approaching a real couple. But they weren't, this was just make-believe. Soon they'd be alone again, and she'd be able to put some space between herself and this irresistibly charismatic man.

'Of course, of course. Will you return to Rome?'

'We will honeymoon in Venice for the weekend, actually.'

Olivia stopped walking, and for the briefest

moment lost control of the vice-like grip she held on her cool exterior. Luca saw, and moved back to Olivia, putting an arm around her waist and drawing her close, so all she was conscious of was the hardness of his physique, the way her side melded to his perfectly.

'A weekend in Venice?' Pietra wrinkled her nose. 'In my day, honeymoons didn't count unless they lasted three months.'

'In your day, it took a month at least to get anywhere interesting.'

Pietra laughed affectionately. 'This is true.'

Olivia was struck by the natural banter between the two, and, despite the happiness of their mood, a chasm was forming in her chest, impossible to ignore. When she saw their easy affection, it was impossible not to dwell on how different her own upbringing had been, how tense and fraught with emotional complications. Only with Sienna could she be herself.

The afternoon light was blinding as they stepped out into the square, and a flock of pigeons flew past them, low to the ground, looking for treats left by the lunch-time crowd.

'Here?' Pietra gestured to a restaurant with tables and chairs lined up on the footpath, facing the square.

Luca turned to Olivia, surprising her with his consultation. 'Yes. I reserved a table. Are you happy to share a drink with Pietra before we leave, *mi amore*?'

My love. Her heart skittled. He was very, very good at this. What was he like in genuine relationships? she wondered as she nodded and they began to make their way to the venue. Undoubtedly, his affection shone as hot and bright as the sun, but, if the gossip blogs were to be believed, his attention wandered faster than you could say supernova.

Her gown was a sleek white silk, ruffled across one shoulder, and as she entered the restaurant the diners paused and then clapped, their excitement at seeing a couple on their wedding day, on the celebration of the great Italian tradition of love, something they couldn't contain. Luca lifted a hand in acknowledgement, and drew Olivia closer, pressing a kiss to the crown of her blonde hair. *It's all for show.*

But that didn't matter. Knowing it was fake didn't stop the very real chain reaction spreading through her—heat seemed to bloom from the middle of her soul, so she was warm and almost dizzy, and desire flickered through her, lazily at first, and then, as he pulled away, more urgently, so she wanted to lean close and kiss him properly, as they had in the church, but this time with no one watching.

He held out a chair for Pietra first, then another. *'Cara.'* He gestured towards it. She swallowed hard as she sat down, aware of his proximity, so sparks of lightning ignited when his hands brushed her bare shoulders. He took the seat opposite and their feet brushed beneath the table—an accident, surely.

Pietra was charming, intelligent, well read and politely inquisitive, asking just enough questions of Olivia without seeming as though she were prying, and the questions were all of a reasonably impersonal nature, so Olivia could answer without feeling that she had to speak to the nightmare that her home life had always been. Conversing with Pietra was a welcome distraction, allowing her to almost, but not quite, blot Luca from her mind. Except there was the subtle contact, beneath the table, his feet brushing hers whenever she moved, so wiping him from her consciousness completely was impossible. He sat back, watching the interplay, taking only two sips of his champagne and a forkful of cake, while Olivia enjoyed a full glass and then half of another, as well as her entire slice of cake. She smothered a hiccough as they stood, and Pietra embraced her again.

'You'll come to Tramonto soon? I would love to get to know you better.'

Guilt was now a full-blown stack of TNT in Olivia's belly, ignited and ready to explode in a confession. She clamped her lips together, trying to remember what was at stake, and that Luca's lie to his grandmother was none of her business. It was the only reason he'd agreed to this.

But misleading the beautiful, older woman felt like a noose around Olivia's neck suddenly. *She's dying.* Sadness dragged down Olivia's heart. There was so much vitality in the older woman, it was hard to believe she was so gravely ill.

'We'll come as soon as we are able,' Luca placated. 'Where is Mario?'

'Across the square.'

'We'll walk you to the car.'

'I can walk myself.' She batted the offer away with an affectionate shake of her head. 'I live alone and still he thinks I can't walk twenty paces without his help.'

'She has an army of servants, in fact,' Luca confided as they left the restaurant.

'I'd like to walk with you,' Olivia insisted gently, linking arms with Pietra.

Luca's eyes met hers and her stomach dropped to her feet. They were going to be alone together soon, husband and wife. She looked down at her wedding ring, diamonds sparkling back at her, and her pulse shifted, lifting, slowing, thready and strong at the same time.

Luca opened the rear door to a sleek black car and Pietra gave them both one last hug before slipping inside. An unknown man—the driver, Mario, Olivia presumed—started the engine and pulled into the light afternoon traffic.

Luca turned slowly to face Olivia and it was as though time were standing still. Her heart began to throb; nerves made her fingers tremble.

'Well, Signora Giovanardi,' he said. 'It's done.'

She grimaced. 'Yes.'

'You're not happy?'

'I'm—' She searched for the right words, words that wouldn't make him sound like a heartless bastard. 'Having met your grandmother, I feel pretty bad about lying to her.'

'Even when you saw how happy we made her?'

'But our divorce…'

'It is doubtful she will live to see it.'

Tears stung the backs of Olivia's eyelids, completely surprising her. She was a world-class expert at hiding her feelings. She looked away, shocked at the raw pain his words had evoked.

'And in the meantime, it's worth it to see the joy in her face.'

Olivia pushed aside her misgivings. 'She must have been very worried about the state of your life for you to have gone to these lengths.'

'I only took advantage of an opportunity that was offered,' he reminded Olivia. 'I would never have married a woman simply to fool my grandmother. But when you arrived, offering yourself to me on a silver platter, how could I say no?'

'I wouldn't put it that way,' she responded tautly. But it was too late. The vivid imagery of her sprawled out on a platter just for Luca's enjoyment filled her mind's eye, and her cheeks flushed bright red.

Luca had no idea what had caused her to react so vividly to his words, but it was clear he'd offended her. Anger glowed in her cheeks, and she didn't meet his eyes. It shouldn't have bothered him but, all of a sudden, all Luca wanted was for Olivia to look at him. Not simply to look. To touch. To lift her hand to his chest, as she'd done during their service, to grab his shirt and pull him closer, to part her lips and moan softly into his mouth.

But wanting his wife wasn't part of this deal. It *couldn't* be.

'This way.' He spoke more gruffly than he'd intended, gesturing toward the doors of a building, pressing a button for the elevator then standing a safe distance from his wife. Maybe it was the dress? Unlike their first meeting, when her outfit had offered only vague hints as to her figure, now he could actually *see* her body, her tantalising curves, could see every delectable ounce courtesy of the clinging silk fabric, so that even before their incendiary kiss he'd felt a jolt of need surge through his body.

The elevator doors pinged open, and they stepped inside, without realising that the elevator was incredibly small. He hadn't noticed when he'd travelled down, but being caged in here with a woman he was doing his damnedest to ignore on a physical level, having her so close their bodies were brushing, was the last thing he wanted.

'I thought you said we were going to Venice,' she enquired, but huskily, softly, and when he looked at her face, her eyes were trained on his lips, as though she couldn't look away. Oh, hell.

'We are.' His own voice was gruff in reply, frustration at their situation emerging in the force of his words. They were trapped by the agreement they'd made. Neither of them wanted this to get complicated, but damn it all to hell if he wanted to push her back against the wall and make love to her here and now.

She blinked, but didn't look away. 'Isn't Venice at sea level?' She swallowed, her throat shifting, and his groin strained against his pants. Hell.

'Sinking below it by the minute,' he managed to quip, despite the charged atmosphere.

'Then we'd better hurry.'

'That's my intention.'

'You're being serious?'

'What about?'

'A honeymoon in Venice?' She formed air quotation marks around the word honeymoon.

'Is that a problem?'

'Well, I mean, isn't a honeymoon sort of redundant?' Heat fizzed between her ears.

'Not if we want to convince the world—and particularly your cousin—that our marriage is genuine. I don't think anyone would believe me to be the kind of man to marry and not take my bride away for a time. We will go, take photographs as evidence. It may matter a great deal, if there is a legal challenge to your inheritance.'

Her lips formed a small 'o', because he was right. It was a small, but likely important, detail, in terms of making their marriage look real.

'*Va bene?*'

Okay? She blinked up at him, wondering why she was fighting this, why she was dreading the idea of a honeymoon with this man in Venice, but unable to put her finger on it.

The doors pinged open but neither of them moved. It was as though their feet were bolted to the floor, as though there were something about the confines of the lift that required them to remain. Olivia felt as though she were about to move into a different realm, as though the moment she moved, everything would change and be different.

A steady, rhythmic whooshing sound broke through the spell, so they both turned in unison to regard the helicopter, with its rotor blades beginning to spin.

The luxury craft had a high enough body that

there was no risk from the blades to either of them, no need to bend down as they approached. 'Are you ready?' he asked, not sure what the question referred to. The small frown on her lips showed she didn't either.

'I think so.'

And despite the fact they'd agreed to a hands-off marriage, it felt like the most natural thing in the world to reach down and take her hand in his, to guide her to the helicopter. The most natural thing in the world to hold her hand as she stepped up, only releasing it when she was seated, and then his own hand seemed to tingle, as if the ghost of her touch remained. Luca had conquered a lot in his thirty-three years, and desiring his wife was just another thing he would need to manage. But the strength of his desire was unexpected. For the first time in his life, Luca felt as though possessing a woman, this woman, was essential to his being. It had never been like this before, even with Jayne, even though he'd loved her. Perhaps, he rationalised as the helicopter lifted up into the sky, it was simply the temptation of forbidden fruit.

Yes, that was all he was dealing with—a simple case of pleasure denied. For a long time Luca had got everything he'd ever wanted in life. Not by accident, but through sheer hard work and grit. Having lost everything once, he'd made sure that would never happen again. As for women, he only had to show a hint of interest before they tumbled into his bed. He had never felt a rush of desire and known he couldn't act on it. Until now.

Understanding himself better, Luca was sure he could ignore the rampant throb of need twisting inside him. He was, after all, Luca Giovanardi, and he'd never failed at a single thing once he put his mind to it...

CHAPTER FOUR

'MY ASSISTANT BOOKED IT,' he explained with a rueful expression on his face, as though this were no big deal. 'I specified the presidential suite, which has multiple bedrooms. She clearly misheard and arranged the honeymoon suite instead.' Both pairs of eyes settled on the enormous king-size bed in the middle of the sumptuous bedroom. Olivia's heart stampeded through her body. Everything since the wedding had taken on a surreal quality, as though with the saying of their vows she'd somehow morphed into someone else entirely.

'I see.'

All she seemed capable of was thinking about kissing Luca. Her lips tingled with the remembered sensations of their wedding kiss, and every second that passed in the same room as him, with neither of them touching, was like a form of torture, a string pulling tighter and tighter until she thought it might snap. But to share a bed? Olivia had never *slept* with anyone in her life. Not in the sexual way, and not in the space-sharing way. It was literally beyond her comprehension to even *imagine* what that would be like.

'I'll sleep on the sofa,' she said with a pragmatic nod. 'I'm shorter than you—by a mile. It makes sense.'

His laugh was dismissive. 'No one need sleep on the sofa, *cara*.' Not just for show, then. The term of endearment rolled off his tongue with practised ease—and that was exactly what it was. Practised. Luca Giovanardi always had a woman in his life, he was simply using the term that came to mind fastest. It wasn't impossible that he'd forgotten her name, she thought with a bitter smile. 'We are going to have to share a bed once we return to Rome. We might as well start practising early.' At her continued scepticism, he lifted his palms placatingly. 'I'm quite capable of sticking to one side, and to making sure my hands do the same.' He turned, taking a step towards her, so their bodies were only separated by an inch. 'I presume you can make the same promise?'

Was he teasing her? 'Of course,' Olivia muttered, heat exploding in her veins. Their eyes met and an electrical current, fierce and obliterating, arced between them. Olivia couldn't look away, but in the periphery of her vision, the enormous, sumptuous bed sat as an invitation, beckoning her—them—to join it.

'Good.' He didn't move. Nor did she. The air around them thickened, holding them still, trapping them, and Olivia couldn't muster an ounce of energy to care.

She badly wished she had more experience with men—but when and how would she have found the opportunity? She dropped her gaze to his lips, wondering how they'd moved so well over her mouth, wondering how he had the skill to evoke such a response in her.

'Olivia.' The word was a gruff command, so she frowned, forcing her eyes to abandon their exploration of his mouth.

'Yes?'

'We agreed to a platonic relationship, but if you continue to stare at my mouth in this fashion, I'm going to want to break that promise.'

'I'm not staring at your mouth,' she denied hotly, forcing her eyes to meet his gaze instead.

'Yes, you are. I am a man of my word, but still a man, nonetheless, with red blood thundering through my veins. You are looking at my mouth as though you can will it to kiss yours, and you were doing the same thing in the elevator.'

'Was I?' Desire was so strong in her cells it left no room for embarrassment, even though she knew she'd feel it—in spades—later.

'Yes.'

'I'm sorry. I didn't mean—' But the words tapered off, the lie failing, because he'd called her out, accurately. It was exactly what she'd been thinking. A furrow crossed her brow. 'I just didn't expect—'

'No, nor did I.'

Her eyes flared wide, his confession surprising her. 'You didn't?'

'No.'

'When we kissed—'

He nodded.

'I didn't know it could be like that.' She lifted her fingers to her lips, as though she could wipe away the sensation. 'It was a charged moment. Our wedding, in front of a priest, saying our vows. It was probably just those factors that made the kiss seem so intense,' she mumbled. 'Right?'

'What else could it have been?' he asked, with a hint of mockery beneath the words.

She wished she knew. She had nowhere near enough experience to say with certainty.

He moved infinitesimally closer, his body swaying nearer to hers, so her eyes brushed closed as she surrendered to the moment completely. 'If it were not for our deal, I would suggest we test your theory,' he murmured. 'But that would be foolish.'

She hesitated, her eyes locking to his. He was right. Foolish. Stupid. Wrong. And yet... 'Surely, one kiss, on our wedding night, isn't such a big deal?'

His eyes flared and passion exploded between them. 'Are you asking me to kiss you again, Olivia?'

She wasn't capable of answering. Her lips parted and then she nodded, an uneven jerk of her head as she tried to reconcile what she wanted with what they'd agreed.

Luca moved closer, and her body ignited, burning white hot with a need to feel that same spark she'd experienced at their wedding. His fingers laced through her hair, dislodging it from the elegant wedding do she'd had styled, his body cleaved hard to hers before he claimed her mouth. It was only in that first instant that she realised how restrained he'd been in the church. That kiss had been passionate and consuming but nothing like this. Now, his mouth *ravaged* hers, his tongue tormenting, his lips mastering hers and disposing of any doubts, his body's proximity tantalising and insufficient. She wanted to feel him, to know him, to touch him, she wanted so much more than this alone.

The kiss stirred every bone in her body, sensuality she had no idea she possessed and was suddenly desperate to explore. He groaned into her mouth and pride exploded through Olivia, because he was every bit as lost to this as she was, as powerless to resist this passion as Olivia.

Her hands lifted to his jacket, pushing at it, sliding it from his shoulders and down to the floor and then her hands were forcing his shirt from his trousers, her fingertips connecting with the bare skin of his toned abdomen, warm and smooth, with a sharp electrical shock that pushed them apart. No, it didn't push them apart. Luca had stepped back as though burned, hands on hips, breath ragged.

'I think we have our answer,' he said, after a moment, the statement grim, as if it were the worst thing in the world that their experiment had failed. Olivia took her cue from him, but her veins were simmering, her mind at explosion point. She was a twenty-four-year-old virgin, she'd never explored this side of herself, never known it so much as existed, and suddenly desire was overtaking everything else. She blinked, turning away from him, needing space to process this, needing a chance to simmer down.

Wasn't a cold shower the legendary cure for frustrated desire?

She moved towards the bathroom with knees that were barely steady, closing herself in and sinking back against the door gratefully. After a moment, she met her reflection and wonderment stole through her. Passion was everywhere, from her swollen lips to dilated pupils, to cheeks that were flushed from the rapid flow of her blood in her veins. She stumbled forward and gripped the marble vanity, dipping her head forward and sucking in a sharp breath. Shower. Now.

She reached around to the back of her dress then groaned once more, this time with frustration. The gown had an intricate system of silk-covered buttons trailing down the back. The stylist had fastened her into it that morning and it hadn't occurred to Olivia to wonder how she'd get out of it again—nor had anyone offered advice, because the presumption had been made that Olivia would have her husband's help.

She tried several times to unfasten the buttons herself, attempted to push the gown over her head, and even briefly contemplated ripping it from her body—only the price tag was still emblazoned in her mind with an element of horror, the cost of the dress shocking to Olivia, who'd been robbing Peter to pay Paul for so long she couldn't imagine what it was like to have the kind of money to simply throw away on a dress like this, and no way would she do anything to damage said dress.

Balling up her courage, she opened the door, catching Luca unawares for several seconds, so she could observe him where he stood, now stripped down to his tuxedo trousers alone, feet bare, eyes trained on the view beyond the window. Flames licked through her. She'd *imagined* him naked more times than she could possibly admit—to herself or anyone—but seeing his bare torso was like a firework display right behind her eyes. She cleared her throat and he turned, as if coming from a long way away, his thoughts clearly distracted.

'I can't take off my dress,' she explained, mortification curling her toes.

'I see.' One corner of his lips lifted with self-deprecation. 'Another experiment?'

'No.' She'd learned her lesson. Hadn't she? 'Just a favour for a…friend,' she supplied awkwardly, because they weren't friends, they were strangers who'd just got married. The tangle she was in didn't escape Olivia, but remembering her destitution, her mother's situation, and most importantly the life Sienna deserved to live, propelled Olivia across to Luca with renewed determination. The ends of their marriage justified the means. She just had to keep a level head while waiting to divorce him. Only thirty sleeps to go… 'Definitely no more experimenting with kissing,' she said, for good measure.

'Turn around.' Oh, God. His voice was so sensual, his accent thick. She squeezed her eyes shut as she did exactly that, staring at the mirror opposite—except that was even worse, because the visage of Luca behind her was like catnip; she couldn't take her eyes away from the picture they made. She tried to focus on the most unsexy thoughts imaginable. She thought of the plumbing at Hughenwood House, she thought of the funeral they'd held for their nineteen-year-old cat, only two months ago, she thought of the day she'd had to leave school to transfer to the local comprehensive, but then Luca's fingers pressed to her back, finding the first delicate button, and all notions but the perfection of his touch evaporated from her mind. She bit down on her lower lip, to stem the tide of sensual need, but it did nothing, and the fact he was moving painstakingly slowly definitely didn't help matters. One button separated, and he moved on to the next, and Olivia held her breath, wanting it to be over at the same time she never wanted it to end. Once the third button was undone, the dress separated enough for her to feel the cool night air on her flesh, and then his warm breath, and goosebumps covered her skin. She was sure he'd noticed the telltale response, because his breath hissed out audibly from between clenched teeth.

'Cold?' he enquired, moving to the next button.

She shook her head. She was hot. Hotter than Hades, burning to a crisp. Their eyes met in the mirror and a tremble ran the length of her spine. She might not have any experience with men, but she recognised the emotion stirring in Luca's gaze, the heat of desire, because it was running rampant through her.

Whether he meant it or not, his body must

have shifted, because his thighs brushed hers, and she had to catch a moan of her own. Her nipples strained against the lace of her delicate bra, painful and begging for touch. Surprise at her body's immediate response, at the strength of her reaction, had her lifting her arms, crossing them over her chest, as if to catch the dress as he unbuttoned it, when really she wanted to conceal the telltale response from him. She was too late though; when she lifted her face and looked to the mirror, his eyes were on her breasts, his cheeks slashed with dark colour, his shoulders shifting with the force of each breath.

Her stomach swooped to her feet and heat pooled between her legs, a rush of need she'd never known before. So she wanted him to touch her nipples, yes, but, more vitally, she wanted him to reach between her legs and stroke her there until the flames were extinguished. But what about their agreement?

Fifth button, and the dress began to droop at her shoulders. Sixth, and the ruffled shoulder slipped down completely, revealing the top of her lace bra. Her first instinct was to hold on tighter, but some feminine knowledge reverberated through her, so instead she dropped her hands to her sides, her gaze holding a challenge when she met his in the mirror.

The dress fell low enough to reveal her bra, and her engorged, sensitive nipples. He cursed from behind her ear, unfastening another two buttons then dropping his own hands to his sides.

'That's enough.' His voice held a strained quality.

Was it? Olivia wasn't so sure.

'I presume you can manage the rest?'

She didn't want him to stop. She wanted to say to him that, actually, help with her bra would be very useful, starting with cupping her breasts then moving to unclasp it, but the sheer strength of her desire was terrifying to Olivia, so she nodded jerkily and stepped forward. Only she hadn't countered on the dress's length, as it had fallen down her body, and she almost stumbled, but Luca was there, catching her with one strong arm, steadying her, holding her for a second too long before dropping his arms to his sides once more and stepping back.

'We'll go for dinner when you're ready.' He turned and strode towards the door, his voice and gait so normal that Olivia wondered if she'd completely imagined his responses to her, if perhaps she'd been imposing the strength of her needs on him. When he didn't turn to look back at her, she convinced herself that was the case—he walked away without a backward glance yet he was filling her mind, her soul, her thoughts and her needs. Thirty nights suddenly felt like a lifetime.

He dragged his eyes over the outfit with a glimmer of distaste and impatience. Having seen her half naked, and in the svelte wedding dress, he wasn't thrilled to have a return to the boxy, unflattering linen numbers, like the outfit she'd worn the night they'd met. But even with the average, oversized drab dress, there was no mistaking the natural beauty of Olivia. She shone like a diamond: stunning, elegant and irresistible.

He stood when she entered the room, noting that she barely met his eyes. Smart move, except her demure avoidance only made his desire increase ten-fold.

'Dinner,' he said with a sharp nod of his head, thinking that what they needed was to be surrounded by crowds, noise, bright lights.

'We don't have to eat out,' she offered. After all, this was a fake honeymoon for their fake marriage. Surely there were limits to how much play-acting he was willing to do?

'Yes, we do, and take photographs as evidence.'

'Right, of course.' He was very good at this, whereas Olivia had naively believed their marriage certificate would be enough to satisfy the terms of her father's will. Olivia moved to the glass doors that led to the balcony, rather than the door to their suite. The waters of Venice's grand canal glistened beneath her, the dusk light casting a shimmer over the surface, and the lights that had already come on in the buildings across the water gave the vista an almost magical look. 'Where shall we eat?'

'Do you have a preference?'

She wrinkled her nose as she tilted her face to his. 'I've never been to Venice.'

'No?'

She shook her head. 'In fact, I haven't been to Italy in a long time—fourteen years. But as a girl, I always loved it.'

'Where, in particular?'

'Florence. Rome.' She sighed, as memories tugged at her. It had been a different time of life. A better time, in some ways, and their occasional holiday abroad had been an escape from the doom and gloom and oppressive resentment that lived within the walls of Hughenwood.

'Did you buy other clothes, at Harrods?'

Her skin paled and he regretted having asked the question immediately. 'No. Why?' She looked down at the dress, and when she lifted her eyes to his face and he saw the shame lining her features, he could have kicked himself for being so insensitive.

'I know, my wardrobe isn't exactly…sophisticated. You're probably embarrassed to be seen with me.'

Idiot. He shook his head, moving towards her. 'No.' He pressed his finger to her chin, ignoring the blade of white heat that speared his side at the innocuous contact. 'I didn't mean that.' *Didn't you? What had you meant, then?* 'I intended for you to have new clothes because I presumed you'd like it. I gather your finances have been straitened in recent times, and that your wardrobe reflects that. The account was set up at Harrods for this purpose, not just for a wedding dress.'

'Oh, I see.' She swallowed, pulling free of his contact, looking beyond the windows, her delicate features concealing a storm of emotions he couldn't interpret. 'Shall we go?' The forced brightness in her tone made him want to eat his stupid question right back up, but instead, Luca nodded, gesturing towards the door.

Out in public was definitely better than here, alone. 'Yes. *Andiamo.*'

The hotel restaurant was beautiful, the food beyond compare, but instead Luca chose a small trattoria a five-minute speedboat ride away, and spent the entire trip trying to ignore the way Olivia's hair whipped her face and her hands flailed to catch it, tried to ignore the desire to reach out and help her, to offer to hold her hair for her, a fist wrapped around those silky blonde ends until the boat stopped and he could tilt her head to his, capturing her mouth once more…

Hell.

The trattoria was busy, just as he'd hoped, the lighting hardly what could be described as 'ambient'. The owner had run the same fluorescents for as long as Luca had been coming here, but the meals were exceptional, proper local cooking, hearty and plain. No fuss, no Instagram-worthy presentation or indoor plants, just good, old-fashioned food, wine and service. As a result, the tourist trade largely bypassed the trattoria, leaving a swell of locals, so the voices that reached his ears were unmistakably Italian. But as they were led to their table, Luca realised the error of his ways. The restaurant was so crowded that there was anonymity in every corner.

'This is nice.' Olivia sounded surprised, and amusement crested inside Luca.

'It's quite ordinary actually. Hardly a romantic honeymoon destination.'

'But this isn't a real honeymoon,' she rushed to remind him. 'Romance definitely isn't necessary. Just a few photos.'

'Of course.' Had he seriously forgotten? Or just been playing along?

The waiter appeared, brandishing two laminated menus and a wine list. Luca scanned the drinks and flicked a gaze at Olivia, who was determinedly staring at the menu. He wished she wouldn't do that. It made him want to resort to underhanded techniques for attracting her attention, like brushing his feet against her ankles as he had at the restaurant, right after their wedding. He took a perverse pleasure out of watching her responses to him, out of seeing the way her cheeks darkened or her eyes exploded with sensual curiosity. But it was playing with fire, and surely he was smarter than that? 'Wine? Champagne?'

'Bubbles, yes. That Prosecco this afternoon was lovely.'

Luca didn't tell her that the bottle had cost almost a thousand euros. He ordered another and handed the wine list back to the waiter, then gave the full force of his attention to his wife. The word shuddered through him like a sort of nightmare. But Olivia was nothing like Jayne, and their marriage was nothing like his first had been.

'Would you like help with the menu?'

She chewed on her lower lip and he wanted to reach across and wipe his thumb over her skin to stop the gesture—it was too sensual, too distracting. 'I should be able to read this better than I can. Even though mum's Italian, she rarely spoke her native language at home.'

'Why not?'

Because Dad didn't like it. She swallowed the acerbic response, reminding herself that their deal included not getting too personal. 'Just easier that way,' she said with a lift of her shoulders.

'Easier?'

'We lived in England,' she reminded him. 'We all spoke English.'

'I grew up bilingual despite the fact both my parents were Italian, and I was mostly raised in Italy.'

She dismissed him with a tight smile, but Luca didn't want to be dismissed. 'She didn't cook Italian food?'

'She didn't cook at all,' Olivia responded with a natural smile. 'We had staff for that, until...'

'Your father died?'

Turbulent emotions raged in her eyes. 'Yes.'

'And then what?'

Her eyes fluttered as she sought an answer. 'And then, my sister and I picked up the reins.'

'Of the household?'

'There was no one else to do it.'

'Your mother?'

Olivia laughed now, a bitter sound. 'My mother has many skills, but housework is not one of them.'

He frowned. 'You were, what, twelve years old?'

'Yes.'

'And your sister?'

'Eleven.'

'And at those tender ages, it was decided that you and she had more abilities around the house than your mother did?'

'You can't teach an old dog new tricks,' Olivia responded dryly, the words spoken as if by rote, leaving him in little doubt they'd been parroted to her often.

'And you juggled schoolwork as well?'

'Not particularly well,' Olivia said with obvious regret. 'My grades started to slip after Dad passed. I changed schools, so that didn't help—everything was new. But there was also a lot to do, which left little time for studying.'

'Or socialising,' he prompted thoughtfully.

She nodded her agreement.

'Anyway, that's ancient history.'

It was, quite clearly, designed to shut the conversation down.

'Have you eaten here before?'

'Whenever I'm in Venice.'

'Which is how often?'

'A few times a year.'

'Why?'

He lifted a brow.

'Do you have an office here?'

'No.'

'Then why Venice?'

'I like it.'

Her lips tugged to the side. 'I'm surprised you make time for leisure.'

'Are you?'

She considered him a long moment and then, as though she were forcing herself to go on, almost against her will, she spoke slowly, purposefully. 'I suppose the women you date expect a degree of attention.'

He relaxed back in his chair, despite the strange sense of unease stealing across him. Why did he want to obfuscate? To move conversation away from his previous lovers? The instinct caught him off guard and so he forced himself to confront it, by answering her question directly. 'Yes.'

She flicked a glance down at the menu, her features shifting into a mask of something he didn't understand. Uncertainty? Embarrassment? He narrowed his gaze, as though that might be able to help him. 'So you bring them here?'

His original instincts surged back, stronger, more determined. 'I can't remember.' He brushed her enquiry aside, even though he knew he'd never brought a woman here before. 'Let me help you with the menu.'

She nodded, a cool, crisp acknowledgement that pulled at something in his chest. He didn't *like* cool and crisp. Not when he'd seen her eyes storm-ravaged by desire. He scraped his chair back, coming to stand behind her, breathing in her sweet fragrance before he could stop himself. His gut rolled; he ground his teeth together. The first moment he'd seen her at that party in Rome, he'd imagined her naked. He'd fantasised about making her his. Why the hell had he thought he could simply switch that desire off? Because he lived for control—and the harder it was to get, the more rewarding success was. He *would* control this.

'Here, there is fried calamari.' He pointed to the menu, his arm inadvertently brushing her breasts as he reached across, and he heard the smallest of gasps escape her lips, so any idea of control ran completely from his mind. He leaned closer, his cheek almost pressed to hers, his arm deliberately close to her now. 'Rice balls stuffed with cheese, spinach and cheese pasta.' He paused, finger pointing to the next item. 'Scallops carpaccio. Do you like scallops?' He turned to face her, his lips almost brushing her cheeks, and he waited.

Sure enough, as though the same invisible, magnetic force were operating on Olivia, she turned towards him. They were so close, he could see every fleck of colour in her magnificent blue eyes; he could see desire in them too, even when they shuttered slightly, her eyes dropping to his lips in that disarming and distracting way she had.

Kiss her.

Temptation hummed in his body. He was only an inch or so away. It would be so easy to brush their lips—but how easy to pull apart? On the two occasions they'd kissed, it had taken a Herculean effort to stop what was happening between them.

'I have to tell you something,' she said quietly, the words just a whisper against his cheek.

'I'm listening.' He couldn't help himself. Luca lifted his thumb and brushed it over her lower lip, so her eyes closed on a wave of anguish, fierce need like a cyclone around them.

'Luca.' God, his name on her lips was its own aphrodisiac. Her voice was husky, as though they'd just made love, as though she'd screamed herself hoarse. He dropped his hand, letting it rest on her shoulder. *Stop this. Control it.*

But was there really any harm in a kiss? It wasn't as if they would be having sex. It wasn't as if they'd be falling in love. If anything, it might actually work to their advantage, bursting the tension that was building between them.

Liar.

'Olivia.' He deliberately layered her name with his own sensual needs, watching as the drawled intonation flushed her cheeks pink.

'This isn't—'

He didn't want to hear what this wasn't. He knew their marriage wasn't real, and he was glad for that, but that didn't mean the passion could be ignored. Perhaps there was a compromise? After all, they were two sensible, consenting adults.

But hadn't he set the ground rules here? Hadn't he been the one to insist they'd never be more than spouses on paper? Could there be new rules?

'I know what our marriage isn't,' he said gruffly, bringing his face closer to hers. 'But I no longer think it makes sense to continue ignoring what it is.'

Her lips parted, and panic flared in her eyes, so he stayed where he was, thankfully with it enough to know that if they kissed now, it had to be her choice. He'd made it clear what he wanted. But would she be brave enough to admit what *she* wanted?

'I'm not ignoring that,' she whispered, her eyes like saucers as she leaned infinitesimally closer.

'Aren't you?' Her brows drew together.

She shook her head slightly, and with the movement, closed the distance the rest of the way. *Almost* the rest of the way, because her lips were still separated from his by a hair's breadth.

'But how—?'

'Do we really need to answer that?'

Her moan was the final straw. It was so quiet, only he could hear it, so sensual, he couldn't help imagining her in the throes of passion. Every cell in his body reverberated with fierce, undeniable need.

'Kiss me,' he commanded.

Another husky intake of breath.

'Now.'

Waiting was its own form of agony. He stayed where he was, even when he ached to claim her lips, to taste them, and this time he didn't want to stop, despite the fact they were in a busy restaurant.

'Our agreement—'

'We can make a new agreement.'

And then, thank God, she caved, mashing her mouth to his with all the urgency that was driving him crazy, moaning into his mouth now, so he swallowed the sound and ached for more. Her hands lifted up, catching his face, holding him there, as her tongue explored his mouth, as she took control of the kiss and he could do nothing but experience her greedy stake of ownership.

This was a terrible idea. He'd known he wouldn't want to stop what they were doing and he didn't. With every fibre of his being, he wanted to strip the clothes from her body and make her his, to hell with their agreement, their deal, their goddamned marriage of convenience. They could draw new boundaries, afterwards. They could do *anything*, after. For now, there was only this.

'Listen to me.' It was Olivia who broke the kiss this time, wrenching her lips away as if in desperate need of air, staring down at her lap. She withdrew her hands; they were shaking badly.

'Listen to me,' she said again, this time reaching for her Prosecco and taking a sip, as if that could erase the urgency of what they'd just shared.

He didn't—couldn't—speak, and so he waited, right where he was, body still close to hers, head bent, desire a tsunami in his veins.

'I've never done this before. I can't just—I don't know—what this feels like.'

He frowned, her words making no sense. He knew she'd never been married before. And he knew she'd never been to Venice before, nor to this restaurant. What was she trying to tell him?

'Are you trying to tell me you're a twenty-four-year-old virgin?' he joked, in an attempt to defuse the tension that was tightening her beautiful lips into a straight, flat line.

She pulled back from him as if he'd slapped her, cheeks glowing pink, eyes not meeting his. His own smile, already taut from the effort it took to dredge up past the storm of passion ravaging him, lost its will, and dropped from his face. He swore quietly, but they were close, so she heard it and flinched, took another sip of Prosecco then clasped the glass in her hands, at her lap.

'Yes.' It was so quiet he had to lean forward to hear the word, but by then he'd already guessed. He knew. He just didn't understand.

He jackknifed up, standing straight, staring out at the crowded restaurant without seeing anyone or anything. His mind was a whir of noise and movement, without the ability to comprehend.

'So when we kiss, I feel things, and I want things, but I have no idea how to—'

He lifted a hand, silencing her. He needed to get a grip on his own emotions. On the one hand, her revelation made him want to put a thousand acres of space between them, on another, it fascinated him, drawing him to her, making him want to teach her, to show her, to be her first.

He moved back to his seat, gripping the back of it, eyes on Olivia the whole time.

She was *so* beautiful. Literally, the sexiest, most stunning woman he'd seen in his life and, given his dating history, that was saying something. How was it possible she'd never been in a relationship before?

'You've never dated a guy?'

She stared at the table, shaking her head.

'You've never fooled around?'

Another head shake, more ignoring him, until she lifted her eyes, finally, pinning him to the spot. And there was cool and reserved Olivia once more—and for once, he was glad to see her. This was a conversation that called for level heads. He sat back down, assuming a relaxed pose he definitely didn't feel.

'Until our wedding, I'd never been kissed.'

He angled his face away, biting back the curse that filled his mouth.

'Why didn't you tell me this before we were married?'

'I didn't think it would be relevant. It's not supposed to be like this. I didn't even think we'd kiss at the wedding—my fault, that was naïve of me.'

'But you agreed to pose as my doting wife, for my grandmother's sake. Didn't you imagine we'd have to share some physical contact, at some point?'

Her eyes showed embarrassment and, inwardly, he winced, wishing he didn't sound so disbelieving.

'I don't know. I didn't—maybe. I guess I thought we might hold hands or something.'

'Hold hands,' he repeated incredulously. 'My God, Olivia, do you have any idea what I've been thinking about? What I thought about the minute I saw you?'

He ground his teeth together, trying to push away the memory of those thoughts, wishing his imagination weren't so damned vivid.

She shook her head, dropping it forward, shielding her face from his, so he wanted to reach across and lift her chin, to make her confront this head on.

But he couldn't.

There were some boundaries they could move. Incorporating a meaningless fling into their meaningless marriage-on-paper was one thing. But there was no way he was going to take her virginity. Not when sex would only ever be a physical act to him.

'I really don't,' she whispered softly. 'But I know what I've been thinking about…things I've never thought of before. My imagination has gone wild.'

'Don't tell me.' He compressed his lips, his jaw almost a perfect square. He didn't need to know that. There were other more pressing considerations. 'Tell me how this is possible.'

'Well, I simply forgot to have sex before,' she said with a tight smile, her joke falling flat, given that neither of them was in a laughing mood.

'You've never met someone who aroused your interest?'

She pleated her napkin over and over. The waiter appeared to take their order, and Luca could have cursed right in the man's face at the interruption. Instead, he rattled off a list of six dishes, hoping Olivia would like at least one of them, then waved his hand in an unmistakable gesture of dismissal.

'Go on,' he commanded.

She hesitated and he wondered if she was

going to change subjects, or suggest they not talk about it. 'It's very complicated,' she said, eventually.

'We have time.'

Her lips twisted. 'It's not important. The details are—I can do a summation,' she said with a little shrug of her shoulders. 'My parents' marriage was a disaster. My mother and I don't have a straightforward relationship. She disapproved of men, dating, in fact, she basically disapproved of socialising, so Sienna and I had each other and pretty much no one else. Plus, I was running Hughenwood House from the time I was twelve years old. When would I have found the time to date? It's a miracle I managed to graduate high school.'

'So what? After that, you stayed home like some kind of modern-day Cinderella, with just your family and chores for company?'

'Don't mock me.'

'I'm not,' he said quickly, shaking his head. 'I'm only trying to understand.'

'I've been asked out before,' she admitted, with pink staining her cheeks. 'But my mother wouldn't have allowed me to accept. And I never liked the guys enough to fight with her about it.'

'And your sister?'

She hesitated, shaking her head. 'Sienna's life is her personal business. I'm not going to discuss it.'

'Fair enough.'

'So what do we do?' Her huge blue eyes blinked across at him, and the answer that sprang to mind was the exact answer he had to ignore.

'Do?' He reached for his own drink, draining it before replacing the glass on the tabletop, then leaning forward, pinning her with the intensity of his gaze. 'That's very simple, Olivia. We do exactly what we said we would at the outset. We remember the boundaries we drew, we remember what this marriage is, and we keep our hands—and mouths—to ourselves. *Va bene?*'

CHAPTER FIVE

SO MUCH FOR being able to sleep in the same bed as Olivia without touching her. It was all he could think of. His whole body was on tenterhooks, wanting to reach out and touch her, wanting to feel her soft, supple skin, wanting to kiss her hollows, to taste her passion, wanting to make her his in every way.

He stared at the ornate ceiling, his pulse running wild in his system, as Olivia slept beside him. Thanks to the Prosecco, she'd fallen asleep as soon as her head hit the pillow, whereas Luca had ruminated on her revelation, on the fact she was completely innocent, until he was crazy with wanting.

But to sleep with a virgin…there was no way he could do it. She had no experience with men, with sex, with the euphoria that accompanied orgasms. How could they remain detached, as they needed to be, if they were sleeping together? He had to be able to walk away from this marriage in a month's time, and to do so guilt free—something he couldn't achieve if they complicated their arrangement with sex. And yet, for all that he'd wanted her before, knowing that she had no experience was an aphrodisiac he hadn't anticipated. He wanted to teach her. He wanted to show her body what she could feel, and he wanted to watch her as she felt her first orgasm, he wanted to go down on her until she could barely think, he wanted to lather her body in the shower then take her against the cold, wet tiles. He wanted…what he couldn't, wouldn't, have.

Ever since Jayne, he'd sworn off relationships. Sex was fine, anything more was where it got complicated. So? Couldn't this just be sex? A little voice pleaded with him, but he ignored it. They were trapped in the same house for the next month—there was no guarantee they could keep things casual. Particularly not given her lack of experience. He couldn't take the gamble that she'd be able to see sex as sex, and not start to want more. It was absolutely impossible.

Throwing off the covers, he stalked away from the bed, finally admitting defeat. He'd been wrong earlier. He couldn't lie with her and know he wouldn't touch. He was half afraid he'd reach for her in his sleep, without intending to, that he'd start kissing her without being aware of what he was doing, and that she'd kiss him back. Because, experienced or not, her body knew what to do, her body understood the chemistry that was flowing between them, and her body wanted to act on it.

Which was all the more reason he had to control this.

With one final look over his shoulder, regarding her sleeping frame with a surge of adrenaline, he left the room, opting instead for an uncomfortable, sleepless night on the sofa— where Olivia filled his dreams, if not his hands.

'What is this?'

Olivia stared in confusion, at first, and then horror, as a parade of not one, not two, but *six* hotel staff walked into their suite, each carrying armloads of clothing.

Luca nodded towards the master bedroom, and they filed in there, each returning with empty hands.

Olivia watched, bemused, confused, but also glad to have something to think about other than the confession she'd made the night before, other than the way she'd blurted out the fact she was a virgin. Certainly other than the way he'd immediately pulled away from her as though whatever he'd been thinking about a moment earlier was now a moot point.

Could she blame him for not wanting to sleep with a virgin? He was used to sophisticated, experienced women. What could Olivia offer him?

She watched as Luca tipped one of the staff, then pushed the door closed behind them, turning to face her, arms crossed.

'Luca?' It was then that she realised they'd barely spoken all day. He'd been working, she'd been pretending to read, anything to avoid the elephant in the room. How in the world was she going to get through the next month?

'You need new clothes.' He shrugged, as though it was nothing, when Olivia had seen the designer names emblazoned on the sides of the bags.

She groaned, shaking her head. 'I don't.'

'You do,' he insisted. 'We're going to have to attend events in Rome, we'll see my grandmother socially at some point. You cannot keep dressing as though you're a kindergartner.'

She flinched at his unwitting insult. He continued to stare at her, his eyes appraising.

'Was it your mother who insisted on this also?'

'On what?'

'Your clothes.'

Olivia looked down at her outfit—denim overalls and a pale yellow T-shirt—then lifted her shoulders softly.

'Partly,' she whispered, not meeting his eyes.

'Because she was jealous?'

'How did—?' She clamped a hand to her mouth. 'I don't know,' she said with a shake of her head. 'Let's not talk about my mother right now, please.'

'When she is at the root of so much of who you are?'

'I know, but...'

'Fine.' He lifted his hands in acceptance, trouble brewing in the dark depths of his eyes. 'Go and look at the outfits. We will have dinner in the restaurant tonight.'

She didn't need to have any experience to know she was being dismissed, but if there was any doubt, it evaporated as he turned away from her and strode towards the table he'd been using as a makeshift desk.

Fighting a dangerous urge to challenge him, she stalked out of the living room, into the bedroom, taking great pleasure in shutting the door as she went. Privacy. Oh, how she needed it!

It took almost an hour to remove everything from the bags. Stunning dresses, evening gowns, mini-dresses as well as casual clothes—designer jeans and jackets, simple blouses, but cut so they were the last word in flattering. She started with the bags on the left of the room, and worked to the right, so it was completely a co-incidence that she left the lingerie to last. But as she opened a thick cardboard box, revealing a ribbon-wrapped, tissue-paper item inside, her heart did a funny little tremble.

It was unlike anything she'd ever seen before. Lacy knickers, ornate bras, and, my God, suspenders. She shoved them back in the box and stepped away, heat radiating through her whole body.

She couldn't wear them.

She couldn't wear half this stuff. It was too beautiful, too revealing, too…

But how could she resist?

Knowing that he'd chosen it for her? That he'd imagined her in it? As if that weren't temptation enough, there was a part of Olivia that had always loved pretty, feminine clothes, a part of her she'd been forced to hide, that she suddenly felt a compulsion to indulge.

Surrendering to temptation, she opened the

lingerie again, withdrawing a particularly beautiful matching set, caramel and black silk. She kept an eye on the door as she changed, then glanced at her reflection, doing a double take at the woman who stared back at her.

And she *was* a woman. A flesh and blood, sensual woman. She took two steps towards her reflection, dragging her eyes over her body.

It was clear that he'd wanted her before she revealed the truth. Did he still want her?

Nothing had changed for Olivia.

She cast a glance over the bed, her eyes landing on one of the more outrageous dresses. It was a sure-fire way to get his attention…and suddenly that was what Olivia wanted most on earth. To hell with the consequences.

She slid the dress on—it hugged her like a second skin—then brushed her golden hair until it shone, pulling it over one shoulder. He'd bought her shoes too, and she slipped her feet into a pair with a red sole and a spiky black heel, pausing to admire the effect in the mirror. It was almost too much. The exact opposite of what she'd been raised to think she should be stared back at her, but Olivia fought the strong impulse to change into something less attention-grabbing.

You only lived once, right?

* * *

If he'd had any kind of heart condition, then Olivia's appearance would have tested it. She emerged from the bedroom like some kind of Venus, a transformation that completely took his breath away. He'd known she was beautiful—hell, she was stunning no matter what she wore—but when she was dressed like this, in heels that made her hips swagger, a dress that hid *nothing* from his appraising eyes, it was all he could do to stay in the kitchen with his hands by his sides.

'Will this do?'

He was drowning. *Would it do?* It would do for him to peel the dress right off her, not to take her out in public. He didn't want the rest of Venice to see her like this, he realised, even as, at the same time, he felt a purely masculine pride in the woman he'd married.

A muscle jerked in his jaw as he grappled with the contrasting emotions.

'Luca?' Her uncertainty confused him. Surely she knew how spectacular she was?

'You're perfect,' he growled, turning away from her on the pretext of grabbing a drink of water.

'There's something important I want to discuss at dinner.' Her cool voice was steady and calm—the exact opposite to how he felt. 'Do you think there'll be a private table at the restaurant?'

He dipped his head. Privacy was the devil— he had to avoid it. '*Forse.* Let's go.'

He didn't offer her his hand as they left, nor did he touch the small of her back to guide her towards the lift. In fact, he walked at least a metre away from her, and when the elevator doors pinged open he kept to his side of the small cube, mutinously staring ahead, refusing to look at her even when his eyes wanted to drink up the vision she made.

The restaurant was busy, filled with Venice's glitterati. Luca saw many people he knew, was recognised, heard the gossip, and also the change in tenor—the surprise at the woman on his arm. Was she being recognised? He doubted it. While her name might be well known, and well regarded, Olivia herself was somewhat of an anachronism. Unlike most people of her generation, she didn't have an enormous social-media footprint, or a paparazzi trail. It was further evidence, not that he needed it, that her life was every bit as confined as she'd indicated. That she'd been a virtual prisoner at Hughenwood House, a modern-day Cinderella, just as he'd charged the night before, left to do chores from dawn to dusk. Did that make him Prince Charming? Hardly. Nothing like it.

'This is perfect,' she said with satisfaction as the maître d' led them to a table at the front of the canal, set a little apart from the others. They were still visible, but their voices wouldn't carry, and that was foremost in Olivia's mind.

While he wanted to avoid being too close to her, Pietra had raised him with faultless manners, so he came to her chair and pulled it back, waiting for Olivia to settle before moving away swiftly, before he could do something stupid like brush his hands over her shoulders. But he did breathe her in, the same sweet, intoxicating fragrance wrapping around him, so he felt himself strain against his pants, as though he were some kind of inexperienced teenager, completely incapable of controlling his desire.

'You wanted to talk to me?' Please, let it be about something mundane and rudimentary. Let her bring up *anything* to take his mind off what he wanted them to share.

'When you agreed to marry me, we negotiated terms for our marriage that would suit us both.'

'I remember.'

'What if I want to change the terms?'

He sat very still. 'Which terms in particular?' But he knew what was coming. He braced for it, for the offer she was going to make, for the test that he was about to meet, no idea if he had the strength for it.

'The no sex thing.' She lifted her eyes to his, meeting his gaze with apparent calmness now. 'I want to lose my virginity, to you. Tonight.'

CHAPTER SIX

HE DIDN'T REACT, but inwardly his cells were reverberating with exquisite anticipation. 'No.' He tried to put a stop to the conversation before it went any further. 'Absolutely not.'

'Hear me out,' she murmured softly. 'Nothing else between us needs to change. I know what you want from me, and you know what I need from you. In twenty-nine nights, we'll separate and, as soon as legally viable, apply for a divorce. I know you were worried that being married might make me develop feelings for you, but I promise, Luca, that's not going to happen.'

'How do you know?' he demanded bullishly.

'Another time, remind me to ask you about the string of broken hearts you've clearly left behind.'

He ground his teeth together. 'I leave women before their hearts can become involved. I'm very strict about it. That is the point.'

'Because of your divorce?'

'Because of my first marriage. Because I have no interest in repeating that mistake,' he contradicted flatly.

'Don't you get it?' She breathed out excitedly. 'We're on the same page with this stuff. Marriage—a genuine marriage—is my idea of torture, one I saw enacted every single day with my parents, and I would rather die before getting involved in that, for real. Believe me when I tell you that the only thing I want in life is my independence. Falling in love would jeopardise that—I'm not stupid.'

His eyes narrowed at the logic of her argument. He knew there were still risks, but her sincerity was obvious. It was easy for Luca to be persuaded by her words. And yet...

'You don't know you'll still feel that way after we've slept together.'

A single finely shaped brow quirked in cynical amusement. 'You think you're so good in bed I won't ever want to leave you?'

He laughed. 'I've never had any complaints.'

'Good,' she responded enthusiastically. 'That's what I want. I'm a twenty-four-year-old virgin, Luca. I want my first experience of sex to be out of this world. Can you give me that?'

'Olivia.' He fought her suggestion with every

fibre of his being, even when he definitely didn't want to fight her. He wanted to scrape his chair back and throw her over his shoulder, drag her right back upstairs and bolt the door shut for at least the next forty-eight hours. How many times since meeting her had he had that fantasy? And now she was serving herself up to him…

'This would still be a business deal,' she said after a beat. 'We're both laying our cards on the table, explaining our expectations. I promise, I won't ask you for anything else.'

He balled his hands into fists where they rested on his knees and absent-mindedly wondered what he'd done in a past life to deserve the experience of a woman like Olivia Giovanardi *begging* him to make love to her.

Still, he clung to sanity and reason, even when the alternative was so appealing. 'You can't say that with certainty.'

'Yes, I can.'

'How do you know?'

She toyed with the linen napkin to her right, then fixed him with a direct stare. 'Because my father was a complete bastard to my mother. Because I saw him eviscerate and humiliate her every day of my life. Because I saw her beg him to love her, and he delighted in withholding that. It is complete anathema to me to give a man that kind of power. To love someone so completely you will tolerate that behaviour—' Out of nowhere, the sting of tears swelled in her throat and behind her eyes, so she tilted her face away, looking towards the Grand Canal while she composed herself.

The waiter arrived at the table to take their order—which Luca placed, handing the menus back then waiting quietly, braced in his chair, eyes tracing the delicate outline of her face in profile. Finally, when Olivia's emotions were under control, she turned back to face him.

'I will never love you, or anyone, and I will never ask you to love me. I promise.'

He felt the honesty of her confession, and it reached right inside him, like a tentacle of ice. He'd never met anyone who'd spoken so calmly about love, and their aversion to it, but her words relaxed him, because it was exactly as Luca felt. Having loved once before, and then suffered through the devastation of that break-up, he had no intention of being so stupid ever again. Could he really trust this was a safe course of action?

'Why did your mother stay married to your father, if his actions were so terrible?'

Olivia's face blanched, in contrast to the fire

in her eyes. 'Because she loved him.' The words were said with arctic disdain. 'We all did. It was only after his death that I began to see things with more perspective.'

'You were still just a girl. How were you to know that the way they lived wasn't normal?'

She pleated her napkin in her lap.

A strange sensation gripped Luca's gut, an unpleasant question formed in his mind and, at first, he resisted asking it. But he was Luca Giovanardi, afraid of nothing and no one, and he wanted all of the facts. 'Did he hit her?'

Olivia's eyes went round. She shook her head.

'Did he hit you?'

'No, no. He wasn't like that.' A tremulous smile tilted her lips for a brief moment before dropping away into a grimace. 'But I would still describe him, if I absolutely had to discuss him at all, as abusive. Financially abusive—he gave my mother an allowance while he lived, enough to maintain her to the physical standard he expected,' she said with withering disapproval, 'but not enough for anything more. She couldn't do anything without his permission—buy anything, travel anywhere. She was his virtual prisoner.'

The original hatred he'd felt for the unknown

Thomas Thornton-Rose grew. 'And when he died, she was still kept under his thumb, by the restrictive conditions of his will.'

'Yes.' Olivia's lips twisted. 'I don't think my mother knew how to react to that. We've all carried on just as we did when he was alive, the same dysfunctional household, the same attitudes, the same restrictions.'

'On you?'

Her eyes met his, and he could see the battle being waged behind her eyes. 'On Sienna and me, yes.'

'Such as?'

She pleated the napkin more furiously now, her fingers working overtime even as her face held a determinedly placid expression—an expression she fought hard to keep in place, he suspected. 'Our father was—'

She broke off when the waiter appeared, brandishing a glass of Prosecco and a glass of red wine for Luca. When they were alone again, he nodded once, urging her to continue.

She hesitated, and he stayed very still, aware that she was sharing something she didn't relish speaking about, but also impatient to understand what her life was like.

'He was strict. I think he was worried we'd

turn out like her, so he did everything he could to discourage that. Where he saw similarities, he belittled them.'

'And are either of you like your mother?'

'I'm her spitting image,' Olivia murmured softly, not meeting his eyes. 'If you were to see a photograph of her in her early twenties, you'd think it was me.'

'And so your father didn't approve.'

'He downplayed looks, generally, while at the same time expecting my mother to dress and look like a beauty queen at all times. It's so hard to explain. Someone like my father is very manipulative—a contradiction in many ways, and a total narcissist. That was his strength. We never knew where we stood with him, nor what would please him.'

She sipped her Prosecco then replaced the glass, running her finger over the condensation.

'For my twelfth birthday, I had a small party— just a few friends over to watch music videos, nothing particularly lavish. But I got dressed up. I did my hair and put on some of Mum's make-up. I'll never forget his reaction.'

She shivered, turning back towards the water, their vantage point affording an excellent view of the exquisite Basilica di Santa Maria della

Salute. It shimmered gold, casting its reflection onto the Grand Canal.

'He was angry?'

'Coldly disapproving,' she corrected, 'but with an undertone of such venom, I've never forgotten it.' She pushed a smile to her lips, as if to change the subject. 'He didn't speak to me for days.'

'What about your sister?' He swerved the conversation sideways, instead, not ready to move on from the matter of her parents, but understanding Olivia needed a break from discussing herself and the ways in which she was parented.

'Sienna?'

'What were they like to her?'

'Sienna is—' Now her smile was genuine. 'She's the most darling person you'll ever meet. She's funny and kind, clumsy as anything, loyal to a fault. Have you ever met a person whose eyes literally sparkled? Sienna's like that. It's as though a thousand stars have been crushed into dust that's been poured into her eyes. She glows with kindness. I love her to bits, Luca.' The intensity in her eyes reached out and took hold of him. '*She's* why I had to do this. Oh, I want my mother to finally be free of my father's oppression, and I want her to have the security of a home, but it's Sienna who just deserves so much better. For all my parents made my life a living hell, it was ten times worse for her.'

'In what way?'

Olivia sipped her drink once more, searching for the right words. 'Sienna and I are total opposites. I'm very like my mother, in looks and emotions, I think. Where my mother and I understood what my father was like, and how to keep our heads low and avoid conflict, Sienna was like…a puppy dog, always bouncing around, looking for affection. It drove him crazy. He came down on her like a tonne of bricks, trying to mould her, to change her.' She winced, hating how it had felt to see that, hating that Sienna could never learn to just stay out of their father's way. 'And so my mother, trying to keep the peace, would be very hard on Sienna, unnecessarily so, criticising her for everything, even things beyond her control, like the colour of her hair or when she gained a little puppy fat. And I—' She swallowed, and now tears did moisten her eyes, so a strange lurching sensation took hold of Luca. 'I'm embarrassed to say it, but I used to be *glad* sometimes that it was Sienna who was in trouble, because when it was her, it couldn't be me.' She screwed up her face. 'I can't believe I told you that. I've never confided that to another soul. You must think I'm a terrible person.'

'You? No, *cara*. I think you're a by-product of your home life, and that you developed the skills that were necessary to get by.' He hesitated a moment, but the moment warranted honesty. 'I think you're very brave.'

She blinked rapidly, to clear her tears, but one escaped regardless, making its way down her cheek. Luca reached over, catching it before it could drop to the table, smudging it over her soft, pale skin, then kept his hand where it was a moment, holding her face, and her gaze.

'No one deserves to live like that.'

Her expression softened for a moment, and then it was as if Olivia visibly pulled a shawl around herself, a cloak of cool distance. 'Lots of people have it much worse. He was never physically aggressive, and we grew up living a very privileged life, as you've pointed out. Hughenwood House, for all it's somewhat run-down these days, is still a stunning country home, with an impressive history.'

She needed to project this image to him, and so he nodded as though he believed her, even when he heard the heartbreak behind her carefully delivered lines. He sat back in his seat, dropping his hands into his lap, watching her with the full force of his concentration.

'I take it this general family dysfunction explains why you're still a virgin?'

Her eyes widened, showing how unexpected the question was. 'Yes.'

He waited for her to continue, probing her eyes thoughtfully.

'You said dating wasn't approved of. Why not?'

'This is really very boring, isn't it?'

'No.'

A plea filled her gaze, and Luca understood it, but he held to his resolve. 'You are asking to modify our agreement. I need more information before I make a decision.'

'I—' She closed her eyes a moment, sucking in a deep breath, and her free hand trembled slightly as she reached for her Prosecco. 'I didn't understand why my mother was so adamant about this. After all, she was married young, and my father wasn't her first lover. How come I couldn't date? But I think—' She paused, wincing, so he waited, curious as to what she might say. 'My mother is a very vain person, Luca. She was always very beautiful, and then my father seemed to value only her looks, so that became what she focused on for a very long time.'

Luca's lips formed a grim line. 'And as you got older, and turned from a child to an adolescent to a stunning young woman, she became jealous of you.'

Olivia's eyes grew wide. He was sure he was right, but some delicate sense of loyalty seemed to prevent Olivia from agreeing with him, so he continued.

'This is why your wardrobe is as it is?'

Heat coloured her cheeks. She didn't respond.

'And she kept you from dating because to see men pay attention to you, and not her, would wound her vanity.'

Olivia pulled a face before looking away. He took her silence as all the confirmation he needed, and suddenly what he wanted, more than anything, was to erase every bit of pain and dejection Olivia had ever felt. What he wanted was to give her *everything* she wanted, to make up for all she'd been denied.

'Are you hungry?'

She frowned. 'I'm—not really, why?'

He stood, extending a hand to her. 'Then let's order room service. Later.'

His final word landed between them and her

eyes widened as his meaning became clear. Later might as well have been 'after', and they both knew what that meant.

It was as though she'd forgotten how to walk, her legs were that unstable beneath her, her stomach in a thousand knots, her blood thundering through her fragile veins so she could hear rushing akin to a waterfall with every step she took. At the elevator, he pressed the button without looking at her, and when Olivia risked a glance at Luca she saw only an implacable, inscrutable face, his eyes hooded, his features set in a mask of determination. A thrill ran the length of her spine even as nerves seemed to be hammering her from the inside out.

This was really going to happen.

Delight and euphoria clipped through her. She fidgeted her hands in front of her waist as she stepped into the elevator, holding her breath as Luca came to stand beside her. The doors pinged halfway shut only to open once more as another couple stepped in, joining them. Olivia stepped back, her bottom touching the metal of the lift wall, and Luca mirrored her step, staying right beside her. As the elevator began to ascend, his hand brushed hers, and she startled as a thousand lightning bolts flashed across her skin. She glanced at his face to find him still looking straight ahead, but this time there was the hint of a smile on his lips and her heart stammered in her chest.

The lift opened and the other couple departed. Olivia's breath sounds filled the cabin. Her skin was flushed from anticipation, her insides all contorted. Her body was wracked with a thousand and one emotions, none of them easy to interpret.

A moment later the doors pinged open to their floor. 'After you.' His words were deep and throaty, throbbing with the same emotions that were rolling through Olivia. She couldn't look at him, and jelly seemed to have replaced her knee joints. At the end of the corridor, he pushed open the door to the honeymoon suite and this time, when Olivia crossed the threshold, she felt as though something fundamental had changed between them. There was an equality to their pairing, an honesty and openness that hadn't been there at first. Inside the suite, she turned to face him, slowly, her eyes round, her lips parted. She'd focused so much of her energy on convincing him that they should do this that she hadn't actually prepared for what that would entail. Nerves began to bounce through her.

Luca held her gaze as he removed his dinner jacket, placing it over the back of a nearby chair, before unfastening the top two buttons of his shirt. He then turned his attention to his sleeves, which he rolled up to just below the elbow, revealing tanned, toned forearms that were, even on their own, erotic enough to make her heart go full pelt.

She reached for the zip of her dress, but a short jerk of his head forestalled her. 'I'll do it.'

Her stomach swooped; her hands fell to her sides. 'If we do this,' he said, something impossible to interpret darkening his features.

'If?' she interrupted with soft incredulity.

He dipped his head in silent agreement. 'I need you to promise you understand the limitations.'

'Haven't we already covered that?'

He seemed to impale her with the force of his stare. 'It's important.'

She suppressed a smile, because he couldn't have spelled things out more clearly if he'd grabbed a white board and started writing it down.

'Just sex. No love. I got it.'

His eyes narrowed. 'When we sleep together, it's simply a biological urge. There's no true intimacy between us, no matter how we make it look to the outside world. When thirty days expire, we will walk away from one another. No regrets.'

A challenge tilted her face. 'That's exactly what I want, Luca. And it's twenty-eight days, now.'

His eyes narrowed. 'And if you start to feel differently, at any point, you promise you will tell me.'

'I won't feel differently. It's not possible. I won't feel anything.'

He seemed to consider that for a moment and, finally, nodded.

'So? Can we do this now?'

He laughed quietly at her eagerness. 'No.'

'No?' She balked at the rejection. 'What the heck do you mean, "no"?'

'You've been drinking.'

She gaped. 'A single glass of Prosecco.'

He moved closer to her, so close their bodies were brushing, his eyes hooked to hers, before reaching behind her and slowly, painstakingly slowly, easing down the zip of her dress. 'When…' The zip reached the line of her bra;

she shivered as he crossed it. 'Not if,' he placated, when the zip had gone all the way. He moved his hands to the off-the-shoulder sleeves of her dress and dropped them, his palms brushing her arms. The dress fell from her breasts and she shivered, her strapless bra a flimsy piece of lace and wire. 'You will be completely sober.'

'I am.' She trembled as the dress pooled to the floor and she stood before him in only a bra and panties.

'Completely.' And yet, despite his words, he leaned forward and drew her lower lip between his teeth, so she arched her back, the contact searing and sensational.

'But I want—'

'You want to learn about sex,' he said, reaching behind her and unfastening the bra, dropping it to the carpeted floor, beside her dress. She stepped out of the fabric, stiletto heels still in place, underpants just a scrap of fabric that could barely contain her heat and need.

'I want to *experience* sex,' she corrected.

'Ah, my mistake.' His eyes showed a glimmer of amusement when they met hers. 'But there is so much to learn before you experience,' he said gently.

'Such as?' Pique and disappointment crested through her.

His hands cupped her breasts when she wasn't expecting it, so her eyes widened and her gasp was involuntary.

'Are you aware you can be brought to orgasm through nipple stimulation alone?'

Olivia found it impossible to answer, but her eyes contained a plea, so Luca laughed under his breath. 'Would you like me to show you?'

'Are you really going to make me beg?' She huffed.

'Yes,' he said simply, moving his mouth to the sensitive flesh just beneath her jaw. 'I'm going to make you beg over, and over, and over again. And you're going to love it.'

His mouth moved from her jaw to her decolletage, pressing kisses along her collarbone before he moved lower, his stubble abrasive on the sensitive flesh of her breasts, in a way that she adored. A moment later, his mouth clasped over one of her nipples and she cried out as a thousand shock waves rolled through her, amounting to a massive tsunami of need. The pleasure was intense. She'd never known anything like it. He rolled her nipple with his tongue, flicking it, then intermittently pressing his teeth down so there was a heady rush of pleasure and pain, a mix of feelings that were hot and completely absorbing. His hand toyed with her other nipple, tweaking it between his forefinger and thumb until she was moaning, panting, barely capable of breathing, much less speaking. He moved faster, then swapped his mouth from one breast to the other, the sensation of his fingers on her moist nipple bringing her close to an edge she couldn't see, an edge she'd never before approached.

'I—I feel—' But the words were lodged in her brain, impossible to locate. How did one describe a feeling they'd never known before? 'Luca, I'm— Oh, Luca!'

He moved faster, and as he plucked and tweaked he brought a hand behind her back, holding her close to him, pressing her womanhood to his rock-hard arousal, so through the flimsy fabric of her underwear she could feel the intensity of his need, and knew that it matched her own. His arousal pressed to her most sensitive cluster of nerves, promising pleasure and delights she'd never known before. Olivia was spiralling out of control, with nothing and no one to hold onto. Except there was Luca, strong, clever, Luca; she gripped his shirt as her world began to change, moving beyond what she'd ever known, becoming fierce and fiery. She held him as she fell apart, sounds of her pleasure filling the luxury suite; her own hips began to writhe, seeking more, needing more, as wave after wave of pleasure wracked her body, redefining her until she knew that the experience had turned her into something, someone, she didn't know any more.

He pulled his head up, his own eyes heavy with arousal as he looked at her, scanning her face as if to reassure himself.

'I'm fine,' she promised. 'Better than fine.' Her hands moved to his belt, unsteady fingers moving to release it, but he stilled her with his touch, taking a step back.

'No.'

'No?' She pouted, still trembling from her first orgasm. 'But I want more. I want to see.'

His eyes sparked with hers, surprise obvious. 'We have a month. There's no harm going slowly, to make sure you don't regret this.'

She ground her teeth together. 'I'm not going to.'

'A few more days to be sure won't hurt.'

'You think?'

His smile lacked humour. 'Not too much, anyway.' He reached forward, brushing his hand over her sex, so briefly, but so perfectly, she whimpered at the subtle contact. 'Please...'

'Tomorrow,' he said, but with firm insistence. 'Tomorrow I'll go down on you until you see stars. *Bene?*'

He deserved a gold medal. A whole goddamned cabinet full of them. He had never wanted to sleep with a woman more than he had Olivia. Every sound she'd made, every whimper, every arch of her back, every press of her womanhood against his arousal had threatened to bring out his not-so-inner caveman, to hell with chivalry. If she weren't a virgin, it would have been a different story. If she hadn't grown up in such a vile atmosphere, been undermined at every turn, made to hide her beauty, made to feel ashamed of it, if she were meeting him as his true equal in terms of experience and confidence, then he wouldn't have let a single glass of Prosecco stop him from possessing her in all the ways they both wanted. But Olivia had lived through hell and the last thing she needed was another man disrespecting her wishes.

But hadn't he just done that? A part of him— his libido, Luca suspected—argued back, just as fervently. She'd clearly articulated what she wanted, and he'd refused to give it to her. No, not refused. Delayed. Besides, he meant what he'd said. There was more to sex than the actual act. She deserved to feel and experience all the things most people did as teenagers, when their hormones were just coming into play and they were exploring and experimenting.

And as she felt, and learned, he would be in control at all times. He would have to be. This wouldn't be like a normal affair, with the sorts of women he usually bedded. He would have to be particularly careful to keep Olivia at arm's length emotionally, to pleasure her by night, but maintain their boundaries anywhere and everywhere else.

Out of nowhere, Jayne breathed into his mind, her beautiful face, her lying eyes, the way she'd looked at him when his father's crimes had been revealed, when Luca had discovered that his once billion-dollar fortune was now worth nothing. And that was how she'd made him feel, too. Like nothing. Nobody. And he'd loved her so damned much, it had felt as if she were stabbing him, or slowly strangling him, the pain spreading through him, only worsening when he discovered she'd had an affair—that she'd used Luca as a stepping stone to climb to what she perceived to be a better marriage, a wealthier husband. And now?

Luca had the last laugh, because he was one of the richest men in the world, and he wouldn't touch Jayne with a ten-foot bargepole. Her legacy had changed his life—he'd learned to keep all women at arm's length, and Olivia would be no different.

He bashed the pillow against the sofa, staring up at the ceiling with a hard-on that wouldn't quit, counting down the minutes until the morning, when her education could continue...

CHAPTER SEVEN

OLIVIA STRETCHED IN the enormous bed with a feeling of contentment that brought a smile to her lips even before she could recall why she felt so darned good. She arched her back and ran her hands over her body, but as her fingertips collided with her nipples, and remembered sensations came screaming back to her, she sat bolt upright, staring across the room at the large mirror.

Heat flushed her body.

Had she really propositioned her husband for sex? And had he really made her feel so incredible with his hands and mouth, and her breasts? Bemused, she stared at her reflection, wondering how she'd never known her body could be capable of such pleasure. His promise hung heavy in the air, driving her feet from the bed. *'Tomorrow, I'll go down on you until you see stars.'*

She could barely contain her excitement as

she ran a brush through her hair and cleaned her teeth, then contemplated pulling on something more modest than the cream silk negligee Luca had bought for her, before realising how absurd that would be considering what she had planned for their morning...

With a heart that was thumping in her chest, she drew open the door to the lounge and stepped out, hoping he'd still be on the sofa.

He wasn't. Luca was, to her chagrin, fully dressed, eating breakfast at the table with the spectacular view of the canal.

'Good morning.' His eyes lingered a little longer than was necessary on her face, scanning as if to see if she had any regrets.

She didn't, and so smiled with extra wattage, moving towards him slowly at first, a strange sense of nervousness that *he* might regret what she'd asked of him.

'Good morning,' she returned, husky-voiced, standing right in front of him.

Their eyes met and held, and electricity almost gave her a shock.

'How did you sleep?'

Really? He wanted to talk about sleep?

'Like a log,' she murmured.

'I'm glad.'

'You?' She arched a brow, unconsciously teasing him.

'I didn't.'

Her laugh was soft and spontaneous. 'No? Why ever not?'

He scowled at her before gesturing to the table, where an array of pastries and fruit was spread out. 'I think, even with your innocence, you know the answer to that. Have something to eat.'

'I'm not hungry.'

His body stiffened. 'No?'

She put a hand on his shoulder, drawing his gaze to her face. 'Not for breakfast.'

'You haven't changed your mind?'

She pulled a face. 'After your very effective demonstration last night? Not bloody likely.'

An arrogant smirk changed his features for the briefest moment and then he stood, towering over her. 'I haven't changed my mind either, Olivia. We take this slow.'

Oh, how she wanted to rail against that! How she wanted to scream that she was ready and to kindly stop telling her what to do and how she should feel, but even as she felt that surge of anger and frustration, she acknowledged the decency of his hesitation. She'd felt his arousal last night. She'd known he wanted her as badly as she did him, and yet he'd resisted. For her. To look after her. The realisation sent a strange wobble into her chest, and emotions of an entirely different sort threatened to overpower her so she tilted her jaw defiantly, employing all the skills she'd mastered in her life of concealing her thoughts and feelings from the outside world.

'So?' she challenged, eyes holding his.

'Ah, yes. I seem to remember I made you a promise last night.'

'Yes, you did.'

'Then I'd better make sure I don't break it. Are you ready?'

How could she ever be ready for such pleasure? How could she ever have prepared for the litany of sensations she'd experience as his mouth caressed her sex, his tongue alternately suckling and lashing, his stubble rough against her inner thighs, his kiss moving from firm and insistent to gentle and slow, until she was crying out, the torture of waiting causing sweat to bead on her brow as flames licked the soles of her feet and she wondered if anyone had ever had a heart attack from the intensity of this kind of passion?

His hands held her thighs in place as his mouth drove her closer and closer to release, and as she began to soar into the heavens his hands cupped her breasts, tweaking her nipples as he had the night before, so shards of delight pierced her soul. His name spilled from her lips again and again, her nails scrambled to dig into the sheets first and then his shoulders, holding tight as she slipped off the edge of the world, into an abyss from which she wasn't sure she'd ever return.

Her breath tore into the room, rapidly at first, like a hurricane, and then slowing to a gale-force wind, until eventually she felt her pulse returning to something close to normal. He stood in the interim, turning his back on her, moving to the bathroom then returning a moment later, regarding her with an expression that gave nothing away.

'I'm starting to feel that this education is a little wanting,' she said, propping up on one elbow, uncaring, in that moment, for her nakedness.

'Oh? Is that a complaint?'

'Well…' she plucked at the sheet, heat spreading through her veins '…it does feel a little one sided.' Her eyes dropped, pointedly, to his trousers, which were still fastened, then returned to his face.

He stayed where he was, arms crossed over his broad chest. 'We have plenty of time.' He held out a hand, and she placed hers in it, so he could pull her to standing. 'Besides, we have plans this morning.'

'We do?'

He nodded slowly.

'What plans?'

'I thought we could tour Murano, seeing as you have not been to this part of Italy before. Their glass is incomparable.'

Her heart stammered for a different reason now, his thoughtfulness wholly unexpected. This wasn't a real honeymoon, and yet he was acting as though it were, and there was a part of Olivia—a large part—that was happy because of it.

Except it was all make-believe; she had to remember that. This was all a ruse, and she had to play her part. 'I've always wanted to see Murano,' she murmured.

'Then get dressed.' But he didn't relinquish his grip on her hand; instead, he squeezed it more tightly. 'Before I change my mind.'

'About that,' she said softly, allowing her own hand to brush his trousers, watching for his reaction. It didn't disappoint. His eyes lowered, his lips parting on a hiss of breath, and then he stepped backwards. 'Murano's been there for hundreds of years. Do you really think an extra hour will make any difference?'

'An hour?' He leaned closer, his eyes fighting with hers, his tone self-deprecating. 'Believe me, *cara*, if you touch me, nothing will take close to an hour.' A frisson of anticipation spread through her at the promise of his words. 'I'll be waiting.' He released her hand and left the room, with Olivia staring after him with a strange mix of arousal, satisfaction and frustration.

Murano defied every single one of her expectations. Brightly coloured buildings stood on either side of the canal, and the sun shone as their boat cruised along the water. Halfway, Luca asked that they stop, handing her from the boat and gesturing to one of the buildings.

'This is one of the oldest glass galleries in Murano. Come, see if anything takes your fancy.'

She walked beside him, happiness and contentment lifting her soul. It only intensified when they stepped inside the enormous ancient yet beautifully preserved building.

'Glass has been manufactured on Murano

since the thirteenth century. The techniques haven't changed in all that time.' He gestured to large timber doors that led to a workshop. The area of creation was separate from the gallery. A handful of tourists was ahead of them, more entered behind, but as Olivia watched the workers below, crafting unique, individual, ethereal pieces, with Luca right by her side, she felt as though they were the only two people on earth.

'They're so skilled,' she commented in awe as they neared the end of the gallery, to a shop where various pieces were displayed, their price tags conspicuously absent.

'Yes. This is a family business. Each craftsman has been trained by their parents, the skills passed down from father and mother to child.' He reached out, lifting a delicate glass. 'It's fascinating how just a few elements can combine to make something so unique.'

She blinked, strangely overcome by the experience, and even more so by Luca's apparent reverence for the ancient skill. She offered him a tight smile then moved away, needing a moment to compose herself.

Shelves lined with glasses, bowls and little trinkets—statues and decorations—clamoured for her attention, so she circled the store several times, scanning the objects with growing admiration. But each time, her eyes lingered on one in particular—a brightly coloured bird with large wings. It stood on a glass base. The whole thing was about the size of Olivia's hand, but every time she passed it she felt a tingling sensation in her fingertips, as though she simply had to touch it. On the third time she passed it, she finally gave in, stopping and admiring it from every angle first, before reaching out and gingerly lifting the piece.

Something locked into place in her chest. Her eyes met Luca's and flames with all the intensity of those the glass blowers worked with flared between them.

'You would like this?'

She lifted it once more, looking for the price. None was visible. 'It's very beautiful,' she said, non-committally.

He reached out, taking it from her, then caught her hand, guiding her towards the cash register, where an older woman was working at the computer.

'Ah, this is one of my favourites,' she exclaimed, eyeing Olivia and Luca with approval.

'My wife chose it.'

My wife. The words were said so naturally,

but they sparked a thousand and one feelings inside Olivia, feelings that she couldn't fathom. There was panic, fear, a sharp need to say 'no', because being some man's 'wife' was something she had always, always loathed the idea of. And yet, in the midst of that, there was surprise and warmth, pleasure at being marked as Luca's. Her nerves tangled, making it impossible to understand herself or her feelings.

'My son crafted this piece. It is a *fenice*.'

Olivia turned to Luca, frowning. His eyes, when they met hers, were appraising. 'A phoenix.'

'Do you know the symbolism of the *fenice*?' the older woman asked as she carefully surrounded the bird in bubble wrap.

'Something about rising from the ashes?' Olivia suggested.

'Yes. In many cultures, the world over, it is seen as a symbolism of rebirth, of hope, of newness.' She taped the bird, then placed it into a brown paper bag. 'He will be safe with you.'

A shiver ran through Olivia at the perfection of having gravitated towards such an ornament. Here she was, taking steps to begin her own new life, and she had unconsciously chosen a symbol of regeneration.

Luca handed over his credit card, a matte black with a silver centurion in the centre, before the shopkeeper could announce the price. Olivia decided she would do better not to ask.

'Thank you,' she said as they emerged back onto the sunlit street. They'd been in the glass factory for over an hour, and in that time the summer sun had warmed so it felt delightful against her bare arms.

They wandered the streets of Murano. The island was not big, and it did not take long, but as the temperature increased it was absolutely essential to stop and enjoy *gelati* from one of the street vendors. Olivia chose strawberry, and the sweetness filled her with a sense of completion.

'Thank you for this morning,' she said as she scraped the last of the *gelato* from the paper cup. 'I've actually really enjoyed our honeymoon.'

His short laugh sent tremors through her body. 'You are surprised?'

'Well, yes, frankly. Don't forget, when we married, I knew very little about you.'

For a moment, his smile dropped, and thunderclouds seemed to pass behind his eyes. 'Except what you read on the Internet.'

She frowned. That bothered him? 'That's right.'

'And still you chose to marry me?' he said as a joke, but she heard the caustic tension in his voice.

'I mean, I sort of had my arm up my back there,' she pointed out, then wished she hadn't when the mood changed completely. Oh, he still smiled at her, but she felt the change come over him, and couldn't quite pinpoint why.

'I thought we'd fly directly to Rome. Unless you have any objections?' he prompted as an afterthought.

The suggestion made her head spin. She was just starting to settle into her honeymoon and now he was suggesting a change? Except, this wasn't really unexpected. He'd said their honeymoon would last for two nights, and it had been that. It was time to go home now. Not to a real home—at least, not for Olivia—but to the place she'd live in for the rest of her very short, very necessary marriage.

'Luca, may I ask you something?'

He regarded her from the back of the limousine with a look that might have scared anyone else off, but Olivia had lived with fear and intimidation all her life, and Luca simply wasn't capable of causing her to feel either. He was nothing like her father. Nothing like she feared all men might be.

'You don't have to answer,' she offered.

'Believe me, if I do not wish to, I won't.'

She *did* believe it. Luca wasn't capable of doing anything *but* calling the shots. She nodded her acceptance of that, flicking her gaze to the window for a moment. Rome whizzed past, the early afternoon light shimmering with that Mediterranean clarity. Ancient buildings stood sentinel to their journey, grey and magnificent, so Olivia wanted to stop the car and go and explore them now, to trail her hands over each, one by one, until she felt their secrets bury deep into her soul.

'Earlier today, you seemed annoyed to think I'd read up on you.'

He was quiet for a long time. She turned to face him, arching a brow.

'I'm sorry, was that a question?'

She could feel his impatience, and something else. A hesitation born of an emotion she didn't understand. 'Yes. *Why* does that annoy you?'

'On the contrary, I think it's a wise precaution. You asked a virtual stranger to marry you. I'd think you stupid not to do a bit of research.'

'Sure, fine, but it still annoys you.'

He drummed his fingers into his knee, his eyes not leaving her face.

'You're not going to answer me, are you?'

He compressed his lips, and she felt a battle raging in his mind, a choice being made. Before she could determine who was the victor, the car drew to a halt. She could just make out a street sign, an old mosaic attached to the building at the corner. Via Giulia, it said. She didn't need to know anything about the street to know that it was expensive real estate. The buildings here were very old, beautifully maintained, with abundant greenery and splashes of colour bursting from gardens that were concealed by high walls.

He waited for her to step from the limousine, before gesturing to a dark wooden door, arched, nestled within a pale pink rendered wall.

'This is Palazzo Centro,' he said, pinning a series of numbers into a discreet electric pad. The door sprang open. He held it wide to allow Olivia to pass. Frustrated at having her question unanswered, she passed without looking at him, and was quickly overwhelmed by the sheer beauty of this place. She had expected something elegant, of course, but not rich with history like this. It felt as though it should have been a museum, and not a home.

'You live here?'

'When I'm in Rome, *sì*.'

'Which is how often?'

The garden was very old, if the size of the trees was any indication. A water feature was set against one wall, creating the delightful sound of rain falling, and in the centre there was a bird bath, with little balls of moss floating on top. A marble path cut through the garden, towards a front door that was timber, with gold detail.

'Most of the time. Perhaps three weeks out of four.'

'And the rest of the time?'

'Wherever I need to be.' He didn't need to push the door open. A housekeeper appeared, dressed in black, her hair worn in a low grey bun. 'Signora Marazzi, this is my wife, Signora Giovanardi.'

The housekeeper did a double take. 'Your wife?' she clarified in Italian.

Luca nodded. 'Please make her feel welcome when I am not home.'

'Certo, certo.' The housekeeper stared at Luca and then gave the full force of her attention to Olivia, who was, by now, feeling a little self-

conscious. The housekeeper's scrutiny didn't help. 'But you are so beautiful.' She clapped her hands together. 'Like a Caravaggio figure with your porcelain skin and luminescent eyes.'

Olivia squirmed under the extravagant praise, a lifetime of criticism impossible to shake off.

Luca reached for her hand. 'We were married only two days ago and will want privacy. Would you see that the fridge is stocked before you leave, and ask the other staff to give us space?'

It seemed to call the housekeeper back to her duties. She blinked, smiling. '*Certo*. I will come back tomorrow afternoon, to see if *la signora* needs anything.'

Luca jerked his head by way of thanks, and Olivia watched the interaction with amusement.

'You know, that bordered on rude.'

He laughed. 'Believe me, Signora Marazzi will be almost as pleased as my grandmother that I've remarried—even if it does prove to be temporary.'

She ignored the tightening in her stomach as his words foreshadowed the end to their ruse.

He guided her through the entrance hall with its vaulted ceilings and chandeliers to a lounge room that was surprisingly modern.

'An electrical fire destroyed most of the house's

interior and the owners could not afford the repair. I bought it for a steal, salvaged what I could, but, for the most part, a total reconstruction was required.'

'Oh, what a terrible shame,' she murmured. And yet, as she looked around the room, the juxtaposition of the ancient stone walls and modern interior had a sort of magical property, as though the house was bridging the gap between new and old. 'It's very striking,' she said sincerely.

'It works.'

'It reminds me of the *fenice*,' she said, with a small smile. 'A phoenix, risen from the ashes.'

He cocked a brow. 'I suppose you are right. I have not thought of it like this before.' His hands caught her hips, holding her still, his eyes probing, asking questions, wondering. She stared back, an open book.

'There are many things written about me on the Internet. It doesn't generally bother me. What strangers choose to opine about me or my family is more a reflection of them than me. And yet, the idea of *you* having read them, of you believing them, is strangely disconcerting.'

Her heart slammed into her ribs. 'I didn't say that I believe what I read.'

His lips formed a grimace. 'Some of them are true.'

'Such as you being a womaniser?'

He hesitated a moment before confirming that with a nod. Jealousy fired through her, fierce and debilitating. She pushed it aside.

'So? Do you think that matters to me? This isn't a real marriage, remember?'

'And if it were?'

She considered that. Would his philandering have had an impact on how she felt about him?

'It's not,' she dodged the question. 'As for your father, do you really think I'm in any position to hold the sins of one man against his child?'

Luca let his hands fall away, turning away from Olivia's penetrating gaze.

'And my first marriage?'

Olivia frowned. 'There was surprisingly very little about that,' she admitted, because she *had* looked. Curiosity had fired her fingers; she'd wanted to understand it—and him.

'No.'

'It wasn't amicable?'

He made a sound rich with disbelief. 'It was far from it.' He turned to face her, speaking mechanically. 'My wife left me for someone she viewed to be far wealthier, far more powerful.

I don't know how long it had been going on, but when my father went to prison, she walked out on our marriage. Jayne wasn't prepared to slum it with me.'

Olivia's lips parted with surprise, and anger. How could his first wife have been so callous? To leave him when he was already suffering so much because of his father?

'She didn't love you.' She answered her own question.

'No.' His lips formed a grim line. 'I came to that conclusion eventually, but it took a long time.' He seemed to rouse himself. 'Her husband did everything he could to rewrite their relationship, to avoid a scandal developing. I had no interest in dragging her name through the mud, so allowed the narrative to play out. There was very little tabloid interest, given the way it appeared on the surface.'

Sympathy softened her features. 'It must have been very hard for you—going through what you did with your father, and then Jayne.'

A muscle jerked in his jaw. 'But I had Nonna,' he said quietly. 'Without her, I cannot say with any certainty that I would have survived.'

But Luca didn't want to talk about his past. He never did, not with anyone, but he felt a particular distaste in discussing it with Olivia. He told himself it had nothing to do with making him look like a failure in her eyes, and everything to do with the vow he'd made himself, to keep her at a distance from him. There had to be some boundaries in their marriage.

But there were others they could disregard. Others they could tear down. Turning to face her, with eyes that glittered with dark speculation, he lifted a single finger, beckoning her towards him.

She dug her teeth into her lower lip as she moved, half gliding across the room, until she stood right in front of him.

Deliberately, with as little passion as he could display, he lifted his hands to her shirt, finding one of the buttons that lined the silken seam. Her eyes clung to his face as he flicked it apart, then moved to the next. Calm, in control, just as he promised himself he'd be with her.

'It's time for another lesson.'

He felt the shiver that sparked through her blood. 'I thought you'd never ask.'

CHAPTER EIGHT

'YOU KNOW, TECHNICALLY that's a revision, not a lesson,' she pointed out, pushing up on one elbow when her breathing had returned to normal. He grinned from between her legs, before pulling himself up the bed, his body over hers, his arms braced on either side of her head as his full weight pressed her into the mattress.

'Complaining?'

'Not at all,' she assured him huskily. 'Just eager for advancement.'

'An A-plus student,' he murmured, nibbling her ear lobe. Olivia held him right where he was, his body so heavenly against hers, his proximity launching a kaleidoscope of butterflies in her abdomen. She could feel his arousal and yet she had no experience, no knowledge, and so, despite his obvious physical awareness of her, worry permeated her fog of pleasure, so her eyes flickered away from his, filled with uncertainty.

'What is it?'

She glanced back at him with a start. Was she so easy to read?

'Yes,' he responded to her unasked question. 'I can tell when something is bothering you. Your face is very expressive.'

'I know.' She expelled a soft sigh. 'I've tried to change that.'

'It's your eyes. They give everything away.'

She grimaced. 'Perhaps a pair of very dark sunglasses,' she suggested thoughtfully.

'Or, you could tell me what's on your mind.'

'Well,' she pressed her palms flat to his chest. 'Actually, that would be you.'

Triumph shaped his features. 'I'm pleased to hear it.'

'Not in a good way.'

'I see.'

'I just…'

He waited, and when she didn't continue, prompted her gently. 'Yes?'

'Is there something wrong with me?' she blurted out, then pulled her hands from his chest purely to cover her face and the eyes he'd just said he could read like open books.

'Wrong with you? What the hell do you mean?'

'It's just, you seem to be able to touch me

and kiss me and make me feel a thousand and one things, then walk away again. Don't you... *want* me?'

He swore in Italian, his eyes boring into hers. 'Look at me, Olivia. Look at my face. Do you not see the tension there? Do you not realise that it is taking every ounce of my willpower to take this slowly, to make your first time what it ought to be?'

Her heart stammered. 'But it's just sex,' she whispered.

'No, it is your *first time* having sex. After me, you may make love to whomever you want, and at whatever speed you want. With them, it will be "just sex". But with me, and for your first time, it is different. Special. Even when we have both agreed it means nothing, it means *something* because you have not done this before. If this were about what I wanted, and what I wanted only, I would have made love to you in the elevator in Positano.'

Her breath squeezed from her lungs. 'Seriously?'

'You think I didn't want you even then?'

He dropped his head, kissing her lips gently. 'You think I didn't want you the second I saw you at that damned party? I watched you and wanted you, even before I knew you were looking for me, *cara*.'

She lowered her gaze.

'So do not think for even one moment that I am simply walking away from you. I am torturing myself by waiting.'

'Torturing us both,' she promised throatily.

'And if I promise the wait will be worth it?'

'How long a wait?'

He laughed before moving his mouth to her breast. 'Not long.' He flicked her nipple lazily, sending arrows of pleasure barbing through her body.

'Do you realise I haven't even seen you naked?'

Heat slashed his cheeks with dark colour and then he pushed to standing, his eyes on hers the whole time. Their eyes locked as he moved his hands to his belt buckle and unfastened it, as he slid his trousers down, as her eyes saw his naked arousal for the first time. Olivia sat up a little straighter, fascinated, compelled, and utterly turned on.

'I—' She was at a loss for words. Helplessly, her eyes drifted to his and stayed locked there as he finished undressing, then stood, stark naked, like an incredibly sculpted statue, a Roman deity, all muscled and mouth-watering. Her eyes flickered lower, across his broadly muscled chest, to his tapered waist, taut thighs, manhood, and lower to his shapely calves. Her heart was in her throat when she dragged her gaze back to his face.

'And now you have seen me naked,' he growled, heat simmering in his eyes, pooling between them. She swallowed past a constricted throat then stood, matching his body language, slowly removing the last of her clothing, until she was also naked in this palatial bedroom with panoramic views over Rome.

The air around them crackled with a challenge, an invitation, and she felt Luca's tension as he decided what to do. Finally, he held out a hand to her. 'Come. Let me show you something.'

He led her from the bedroom, down the corridor, both as naked as the day they were born.

'What about Signora Marazzi?'

'What about her?'

'What if she sees—?'

'I suspect she left almost immediately.'

'I suppose she's used to your philandering

habits.' Olivia giggled softly, wondering why the sound was oddly forced to her own ears.

He threw a glance over his shoulder. 'This way.'

She noticed he didn't respond to her statement. Well, so? What could he say? They both knew the lie of the land—he was a bachelor, through and through. Nothing about this was new for him, except the whole 'marriage' part, and even then, he'd been married before. Something rolled through her, something dark and fierce, surprising her. It was a mix of curiosity and something else, something fiercer, compelling her to understand about his first marriage, about his life before her, about the experiences that had shaped him. But that was none of her business. Per their agreement, she had no right to ask, and certainly, no expectation that he'd answer.

The hallway opened onto a landing and a narrow set of stairs. She followed behind his naked form, admiring the muscled firmness of his rear as he moved up two flights then pushed a modern steel door open. They burst onto a rooftop terrace, shielded from view by hedges that grew in large terracotta pots. At the centre of the paved terrace was a pool, submerged, and the most striking turquoise colour Olivia could imagine. The afternoon sun bounced off it tantalisingly, invitingly, so she glided towards it on autopilot.

'How stunning,' she murmured, not realising that Luca had followed. He placed his hands on her hips, drawing her back against him, so his arousal pressed between her buttocks. She closed her eyes on a rushed gasp, her pleasure only increasing when he brought one hand around to her breasts, lazily stroking her nipples before moving his mouth to the crook of her neck, whispering and tasting her there until she was moaning softly into the afternoon sun.

'Swim with me,' he suggested.

She wanted to do so much more than swim with him, but when he released her and dived into the water, she stood there, watching his lithe athleticism, spellbound by his masculine beauty, before she did the same, splashing into the water with a heady sense of euphoria. Her wedding ring glinted as she swam, catching her eye, the diamonds so clear and sparkling.

It was a sign of possession she'd always railed against, but on this day, in this minute, wearing this man's ring, Olivia couldn't say she minded, at all.

* * *

'That was incredibly delicious.' She dabbed her lips with the linen napkin, then placed it in her lap.

'Signora Marazzi is an exceptional cook,' he agreed.

'Does she make all your meals?'

'Or I eat out.' He shrugged.

'You never cook for yourself?'

'No. I never learned.'

'It's not rocket science.'

'Perhaps. But there's no need.'

'What about during your marriage? Don't tell me your wife was chained to the kitchen?'

'Hardly,' he drawled, without elaborating further. The same curiosity that had burst through Olivia earlier that day flooded her again.

She leaned forward. 'You don't have to answer if you don't want to.' It was a silly precursor to say—naturally Luca wouldn't do *anything* he didn't want to. 'When your wife left you, you went to live with your grandmother?'

'That is no secret,' he said, quietly though, warily, as though he was bracing for an even worse question.

'She wasn't affected by the bankruptcy?'

'He's her son.' Luca's voice was strained. She

reached over and pressed her hand to his. 'Of course, she was affected.'

'I meant in a financial sense.'

His smile held a rejection. 'My grandmother owns her own house, and her own business. When my father inherited from my grandfather, it was always on the basis that Nonna's assets would be held separate. There was no threat to her.'

'What a wise precaution that turned out to be.'

'My grandfather insisted. Nonna came from nothing, and he always joked that it was the only way he could be sure she really loved him. He made her a very wealthy woman even before he proposed, so he knew there was no financial incentive in her accepting the proposal.'

'He was a cynic?'

'Or a realist. He was worth a small fortune.'

'She obviously loved him.'

'She did. But even once they were married, her fortune was kept aside, all in her name, all her own. So when my father was charged, and everything he owned was taken away, Nonna lost nothing.'

'Except her son,' Olivia murmured sadly.

'And her good name,' he added. 'Thanks to my father, Giovanardi now means "mud" in Italian.'

Olivia winced. 'You don't deserve that.'

'Don't I?'

She pulled her lips to the side, shaking her head a little. 'Of course you don't. None of it was your fault.'

He placed his knife and fork on his plate, glaring at them. 'I wish things had turned out differently.'

'Do you speak to him?'

'No.'

'Your choice or his?'

'Mutual.'

'You haven't forgiven him?'

'Not really. And I know he'll never forgive me.'

'Why? What did you do that was so terrible?'

Luca's eyes met hers, almost as though he was challenging her to think as badly of him as he did himself. 'I caused it all, *cara*. It's my fault.'

'What are you talking about?'

'I discovered what he'd done. I couldn't fathom how he'd dug such a deep hole, and so I confronted him, hoping for a simple explanation. Only the one he gave made no sense. I could see there was never going to be a way to pay off all the investors. It was a Ponzi scheme, an enormous house of cards, ready to tumble at the slightest breeze.'

She grimaced. 'It must have been terrible for you to realise that.'

'He preyed on our friends, the parents of my school friends, men he'd known all his life. He was unscrupulous and greedy. When I went to the police, it was in the hopes some of the money could be recovered, but the scheme collapsed and everyone lost everything.'

'You most of all,' she said quietly.

He ran a hand through his hair. 'We were very wealthy, but it wasn't enough for him. He wanted more, always more.'

Olivia couldn't offer any words to comfort him, so she did the only thing she could, moving around the table and settling herself on his lap, arms hooked behind his neck.

'That isn't your fault.'

He met her eyes, and she saw the trauma in them, the regret, the fervent wish that things had been different. How she ached for him!

'Not your father's actions, nor your wife's betrayal. You didn't deserve any of it.'

He kept his gaze averted from hers, a muscle throbbing low in his squared jaw, so she lifted a finger to it, feeling his pulse, fascinated by the tightness there as he clenched his teeth together.

'How did you do all this?' She shifted the subject a little, waving a hand around her to the palatial lounge that opened onto the back garden. 'You rebuilt an empire from nothing.'

'Not nothing,' he corrected with a bitter smile. 'There was Nonna's business.'

'She handed it to you,' Olivia guessed.

'Yes.' His expression was defiant. 'She trusted me, and I desperately wanted to make her proud, to prove her right. I worked around the clock for two years, growing her small chain of accommodation into a global force of exclusive, boutique hotels, before branching out into transport logistics, and then airlines. It wasn't easy. None of the major banks in Italy would, initially, lend to me.' A cynical smile tilted his lips. 'Including Azzuri—the bank I plan to acquire.' The rejection had been one of many he'd experienced at the time, but it had cut him deep, representing what he'd thought to be the end of the road. The humiliation he'd felt, at having to go in there to beg, in the first instance, and having his proposal tossed out as though it were worthless junk. He'd never forgotten that humiliation.

'Even with your grandmother's wealth?' Olivia stroked his cheek gently.

'Even then.' Luca brought himself back to the present. 'Giovanardi means mud, remember?'

'What did you do?'

'Sold two of her hotels to raise capital.'

She shook her head. 'You must have been so scared.'

His lips twisted in a mocking smile. 'Angry, actually.'

She laughed softly. 'Yes, that too.'

'I hated the banks, all of them. And particularly Azzuri,' he was surprised to hear himself admit. 'It was when I expanded into new tech that things really improved. I was able to pay back my father's debts—every last one of them—and to create an empire my grandfather would have been proud of.'

She heard his drive and determination, and the dark forces that had compelled him to work so hard for so long, and felt a surge of pity. Would he ever feel that he'd done enough?

'Pietra must have been impressed.'

His smile was just a hint. 'Yes.' He lifted a hand to Olivia's cheek, tucking her hair behind her ear. 'She'd lost so much. My grandfather, then the family reputation, the business. I knew that I couldn't fail her.'

'You didn't.'

He dipped his head in acknowledgement. 'And yet,' he said quietly, 'it doesn't matter how much I am worth, or how much business succeeds, there is always a question hanging over my head. Did I cheat to get here? Am I like my father? Can people trust me? His shadow has dogged me my entire adult life.'

She shook her head a little. 'And yet, look at my father—a man whose ancient name earned him a seat at any table, who was thought of so highly, and yet, he was—as you said—a total jackass.' She leaned closer, her gaze intense. 'What does a name matter, Luca? It's the man that counts, the man you are, the deeds that you do. That's what people should care about.'

She ran her finger around his lips, tracing the outline there. 'And I think you are a good man, who's done great deeds. In fact, I think you're very noble.'

'Because I married you?' he prompted, his voice lightly teasing.

'Absolutely,' she responded in kind, only half joking, then sobered. 'You saved me. I mean that seriously.' Tears threatened so she forced a bright smile. Things were getting too serious between them, too intense. Neither of them wanted that. 'And because you paid back the money your father stole, when you didn't have to.'

'Not legally, but morally. Ethically.'

She brushed her lips over his. 'See? You're undoubtedly decent.'

He expelled a short sound of amusement. 'I don't think you'd say that if you knew the decidedly indecent thoughts I've been having about you.'

Pleasure warmed her. 'Tell me,' she invited, moving her bottom a little from side to side, watching as his eyes darkened with the unmistakable rush of desire. 'Or better yet…' She moved her mouth to his, kissing him gently at the corner. 'Show me,' she invited, pushing his shirt up his body, revealing his taut abdomen, her fingers brushing his wall of abdominals then discarding the shirt on the floor. He didn't fight her and she was so glad; she didn't realise *how* sure she'd been that he would fight her until he didn't and relief flooded her body. Relief, and a rush of desire.

She shifted on the seat, needing more purchase, more of him, so she lifted up and straddled him, allowing her head to drop to his chest, her tongue to tease his nipples, as he'd done to her on so many occasions. He shuddered beneath her touch, pleasure radiating through him, so power surged in her veins.

'Are you sure you want to do this?' he asked, and hope was an explosion in the centre of her chest.

'Do what?' she prompted with mock innocence, blinking her blue eyes at him.

He groaned, bringing his hands to cup her buttocks, drawing her right onto the hardness she could feel through his trousers. The smile dropped from her mouth as urgency overtook her.

'I'm sure,' she agreed. 'Did you think I'd change my mind?'

'I don't know.' His smile was taut. 'You only get one chance to lose your virginity.'

'Do you think I want to wait until I'm thirty?'

'I think you might want to wait until you meet someone you're in an actual relationship with.'

'We've discussed that.' She shook her head resolutely. 'I'm no more interested in an actual relationship than you are.' Saying those words felt good. Important. Because they also felt very wrong, and she couldn't understand why, but she needed to hold onto their agreement, the pledge they'd made to one another. 'I'm only after meaningless sex, remember?'

She moved back to kissing him, need propelling anything else from her mind. It was the same for Luca. Having held off for days despite the temptation, he felt, finally, as though he were about to be unleashed and his impatience knew no bounds. He undressed Olivia as quickly as he could, not wanting to move her from his lap but needing better access to lower her pants. God, if it weren't her first time, he'd have loved to make love to her right here, like this, with her on his lap at the dining table, God help him, it would be perfection. But not for her first time.

He stood, lifting her easily, wrapping her legs around his waist as he carried her through the house, up the stairs to his bedroom, his fingers kneading her buttocks.

'I can walk,' she said on a tremulous laugh, her voice brushing his throat.

'And then I would not get to hold you like this.'

His bedroom felt like a thousand miles away. Finally, he shouldered his way through the door and placed her on the bed, bringing his body over hers, not pausing to draw breath, just needing to kiss her properly now that he could. Her hands roamed his naked torso, feeling, touching, exploring, familiarising herself with him completely; he'd never known something as simple as touch to be so incendiary. He stepped out of his pants with urgency, needing to be naked and close to her, needing her with a fire-like intensity.

Her fingers glided down his arms, latching with his, so he held her arms at her sides as he kissed her, devouring her, passionately possessing her until he pushed her back onto the bed and they fell, a tangle of limbs, legs entwined and writhing as they sought the ultimate closeness. His need for her cracked through him, contorting him, so he had to focus to remember her innocence, to hold himself back, to stop from taking her as he wanted.

But at every step, Olivia met him as an equal, so that despite her innocence she was his match, her enthusiasm giving her confidence. But it was more than that. Holding back, waiting for this, exploring each other day after day, had built to a crescendo. They'd been engaged in a torturous form of foreplay for days and nights, desire building until it reached a zenith. Her touch drove him wild, driving all ability to think from his mind. She wrapped her legs around his waist, drawing him closer, and the tip of his arousal nudged between her legs, so he groaned, long and low, aching to push into her, to feel her muscles spasm around his hard length. But caution was ingrained in Luca, so even now, while incapable of stringing two words together, he knew enough to pull up and take a moment, to stare down at her, before reaching to his bedside table and removing a condom. His eyes latched to hers as he opened the packet, then slid it over his length—an act Olivia's own gaze devoured in a way that made desire spear him from the inside out. 'Do you have any idea what you're doing to me?'

'Me?' She purred.

He laughed gruffly. 'Oh, you know *exactly* how you make me feel.'

She reached up, grabbing him by the shoulders so she could pull him back on top of her. 'Maybe a fraction of how *you* make *me* feel?'

'Is that a fact?'

'I think it might be.'

'And what about this?' He pressed himself inside her, just enough for Olivia to gasp, her eyes widening, so confused wonder crossed her features.

'Are you okay?'

She nodded, her features tense.

'Breathe,' he said gently, lowering his mouth to hers, brushing their lips as he pushed into her completely, slowly at first, giving her time to adjust to the invasion of his arousal.

Olivia tensed as pain gripped her, unexpected, immediate, but searing, like a flash of lightning in the sky, and then it was gone, giving way to slight discomfort at first, and then a warm glow of pleasure as he began to move, his arousal so deep inside her that she felt a pleasure she'd never known possible. He kissed her in time to his movements and she scratched her fingers down his back as euphoria threatened to overtake everything else.

Only the sound of her rushing blood filled Olivia's ears. She would never have said pleasure could be excruciating but, to her, that was what it felt like, as each thrust of Luca's arousal seemed to bring her both pleasure and impatience all at once. Stars formed behind her eyelids and then, out of nowhere, she was bursting apart at the seams, pleasure no longer excruciating but almost too exquisite to bear. She rolled back her head and squeezed her eyes shut as she rode the wave of release, his name on her lips, filling the silence of the room, adding to the cacophony of her own body's pleasure.

He pushed up on one elbow, scanning her eyes as if seeking reassurance, and when Olivia's breath slowed, she smiled at him, wonder and joy in her features.

But it was only a temporary reprieve and then Luca was moving again, and now his possession was hard and fast, showing Olivia how gentle he'd been the first time, how deferential to her inexperience. Pleasure had built quickly, but it was nothing compared to this. As he thrust into her again, and again, hard and fast, a primal, animalistic need spread like wildfire, so she was pushing up and rolling over, needing to be on top, to take more of him, all of him.

He growled, a low, husky sound, as he grabbed her hips, holding her deep on his length for a moment, then letting go, so Olivia controlled the rhythm, bucking and rolling hard and fast at first then moaning softly as she slowed down. His hand brushed her sex, his fingers pressing her there until the combination of his possession and his touch was too much, and she was tumbling again, over the edge of reality, into a field of utter heaven. But this time, she wasn't alone. Luca lifted his hips, taking control once more, and then he was joining her, exploding as he said her name, then pulled her down towards him, kissing her as his body was wracked with his exploding pleasure, kissing her as both morphed into something beyond what they could recognise.

'So, that's sex, huh?' She pushed up a little, to see into his eyes. Pleasure still throbbed between her legs, and she was glad he stayed inside her; she wasn't ready to lose that intimacy yet.

'Pretty much,' he responded in kind, light-hearted, both somehow understanding that they needed to contrast the intensity of what they'd just shared with the casual nature of their relationship.

'Well, I'm not sure I see what all the fuss is about,' she said with obvious sarcasm, her body still trembling with the force of her release.

He laughed softly, caught her wrists then rolled them, pinning Olivia on her back beneath him, pulling out of her so she moaned, wanting him back more than anything. 'Then perhaps you need another demonstration?'

She batted her eyelids, pretending to consider

it. 'That could be useful,' she said after a lengthy pause.

'Minx.' But he laughed for as long as he was able, before taking one of her nipples in his mouth and biting down on it, hard enough to make her moan. Olivia lifted her hips, surrendering to the hedonism of this, and in the back of her mind, in the small part of her brain capable of rational thought, she was aware of how fortunate she was. She'd married a man who was teaching her the pleasure her body was capable of feeling, and in a few weeks, they'd walk away from one another—no hard feelings. It was everything she hadn't known she'd wanted, until she'd married Luca Giovanardi.

CHAPTER NINE

'HANG ON. WHAT are you wearing?'

He turned to face her, a sardonic look of enquiry on his face that made her simmer with
desire. 'Brioni, I believe.'

'A suit? But whatever for?' After all, in the
week since their first time together, Olivia and
Luca had barely left bed, except to eat or swim,
and even then they'd been naked.

'I have a meeting and I'm pretty sure, though
not one hundred per cent, that nudity would be
frowned upon.'

'A meeting? With other people?' She reached
out a hand, drawing him to her, her eyes an invitation Luca couldn't resist.

'With the chairman of Azzuri Bank, in fact.'

Olivia tilted her head to the side, considering that. He'd only mentioned it briefly, but she
hadn't forgotten the fierce look of determination that had gripped him as he'd referred to
the bank that had refused to lend money to him

when he'd been starting over in life. She knew what this meeting would mean for him.

'I've been out of the office way longer than intended,' he continued, conversationally. Calm. In control. Just like always.

'I'll take that as a compliment.'

'As it was intended.' He pressed a kiss to the tip of her nose, aware that if he didn't pull away from her, he'd start undressing, adding a delay to his schedule he couldn't afford. 'You have no need to do anything so horrible as pull on clothing. In fact, I'd suggest you don't.'

A smile tipped her lips. 'Oh? What shall I do all day, then, Luca?'

'Lie naked in bed and wait for me.' He grabbed her hand, pressing it to her sex. 'Think of me. Miss me.'

Her heart stumbled and pleasure burst through her, but it was quickly followed by a surge of panic so fierce it took all her energy to conceal any display of it. Wait for him? Think of him? *Miss him?* What happened to the independence she was fiercely chasing? To never wanting to be like her mother, so stupidly loyal and in love she forgave Thomas anything and everything?

Olivia angled her face away on the pretence of scoping out the weather. 'It's sunny again today. I might go and explore. I fear clothes will be necessary for me, too.'

'My driver can take you anywhere,' he offered, after a slight pause.

'I'd prefer to walk.'

He lifted his shoulders in a shrug then straightened. She didn't fight his departure—she'd had a wake-up call and it had been a vital, timely reminder. Do *not* depend on him. Do *not* ask him for more.

'Suit yourself. Don't get lost.'

He moved to the door, all casual, breezy, noncommittal, so she felt silly for having experienced a sense of panic. They were nothing like her parents. This was nothing like their marriage. Olivia would *never* be beholden to another person as Angelica had been Thomas.

And yet, a powerful need to underscore that drove through her, so she called to him, when he was almost out of the door. 'Only three weeks to go, Luca. Let's make the most of them.'

It was the affirmation she needed, words that were a balm to her soul, even when they pulled at something in her chest, leaving her scrambling, a little, to draw sufficient breath. Life after Luca loomed, and she no longer knew exactly what shape it would take.

* * *

It was precisely because he was thinking of Olivia almost constantly that Luca remained at his desk until after seven, that evening. He was getting close to securing the deal of the century. It wasn't final yet, but he finally had the support of the chairman of the Azzuri Bank. It had taken years of delicate negotiations, but he'd done it, and there was vindication in his success. Revenge, too. Because they kicked him while he was down, and he'd sworn he'd never forget it.

He hadn't.

And now the bank would be all his; he was sure of it.

It should have been all he could think of, the success of his day's meetings monopolising his thoughts, but instead, Luca found his mind wandering to Olivia, obsessing over his memories of her in his bed, of the way she'd looked when he'd left, so beautiful, so distracting.

While it was true that he had mountains of work to catch up on after his spontaneous wedding, honeymoon and protracted post-honeymoon holiday here in Rome, and that his time was therefore very well spent in the office, it was far more accurate that he was challenging himself to resist her. Or, proving to himself that, after a week spent almost exclusively in bed, she had no greater hold on him now than she had on the first day they'd met. That was to say, she was a woman he found desirable, that he enjoyed sleeping with, who he'd walk away from without a backwards glance when the time came. And the time would come—more surely than in any previous tryst—because they'd agreed on that. Three more weeks of Olivia, and then she'd be gone from his life, just as they both wanted.

Having worked late, Luca had every expectation that Olivia would be at home when he returned. He was so sure of it that he'd already started fantasising about how it would feel to pull her into his arms and strip the clothes from her body, to kiss her until she was a puddle of desire, begging him to make love to her. He stormed into the palazzo, already hard, wanting her with a strength that should have terrified him. But it didn't, because this was simple and clear-cut—they both knew what they needed from this relationship.

Only, Olivia wasn't home, and the frustration that gripped him was dark and intense. He stopped walking, having inspected the house thoroughly, a frown on his handsome face. He contemplated heating himself some dinner, going for a solo swim, just as he would have in his pre-Olivia life, but her parting words still rang in his ears.

'Only three weeks to go, Luca. Let's make the most of them.'

He reached into his pocket and drew out his cell phone, dialling her number then pressing the speakerphone button, so he could begin removing his work clothes as the phone rang. She answered on the fourth ring.

'Luca, hi.'

Her voice wrapped around him like tendrils from the deep sea, threatening to drag him under. He pressed his hand to the wall, emulating a nonchalant pose.

'Where are you?'

The sound of laughter filled the phone, distant and remote.

'Out at dinner.'

'With whom?'

'Myself.'

'Why?'

'You weren't home. I presumed you were busy, and I was hungry.'

'The freezer's full.'

'When in Rome, do as the Romans do. And

I took that to mean, eat out,' she said, so he could just picture her slender shoulders shrugging with casual indifference. Hunger flicked through him.

'I haven't ordered yet. Why don't you join me?'

He jerked his head once in silent agreement. 'Text me the name of the restaurant. I'll see you soon.'

She might not know the city, but Olivia had exceptional taste. She'd opted for one of the most adored restaurants in Rome. Not the fanciest, nor the predilection of the glitterati, but a place where true Romans who loved good food, wine and conversation chose to eat. And because the owner Francesco understood the value of placing beautiful patrons in the windows, Olivia had been afforded a prominent table in the centre of the glass that framed the front of the venue.

Luca approached slowly, his eyes picking her from a distance, and, owing to the fact he was coming from across the street, he had several moments to observe her while she studied the menu, a small frown on her stunning face.

She wore a black dress, simple yet elegant, with cap sleeves and a neckline that was low enough to show the smallest hint of cleavage. The dress was fitted to her waist then flared a little, to just above her knees. Her blonde hair was left out, slightly curled, and she'd applied a coat of red lipstick, completing the look of femme fatale. She was beyond beautiful; she was exquisite, a completely unique woman who was impossible to ignore. Indeed, as he moved closer, he was aware of the table behind her—a group of four men on what looked to be a business dinner—casting lingering glances in her direction, appreciating her in a way that made Luca's blood boil.

But he stamped out that reaction before it could take hold.

He had no right envying her that kind of attention. Theirs was not a real marriage, and whatever they were sharing was a very temporary state of affairs. Sleeping together didn't equate to anything more serious—they both knew that—and he was glad. If anything, it was useful to observe her like this, to see her from outside the restaurant. The symbolism didn't escape him. A physical barrier stood between them, and in a few weeks that physical barrier would be a whole other country, and then, something more significant—a divorce. Soon, they'd be strangers, just memories to one another.

As that thought hardened in his mind and heart, she looked up, her eyes landing on him, widening, before a smile curved her perfect, pouting lips.

'Hello,' she mouthed.

His own grin was slow, and felt a little discordant, but she didn't appear to notice. With a graceful shift of her hand, she indicated the chair opposite, wordlessly inviting him inside, to join her. His gut tightened with something like anticipation and then he nodded, pushing into the restaurant. *Let's make the most of this.*

'*Buonasera,*' she greeted him as he approached her table.

He dipped towards her, pressing a kiss on her cheek, lingering there longer than necessary so he could breathe her in and placate nerve endings that were firing wildly, desperate for her, for more, for everything.

'*Ciao.*'

He slid into the seat opposite, grateful that the table was small and intimate, that their knees brushed and that neither shifted to break that connection. But why would they? They'd been far more intimate than that, and yet the small contact sent a thousand flares through his body.

'How was your day?'

He'd been floating on air after leaving the office, the success of his meeting with the Azzuri chairman puffing out his chest. But there was a light behind Olivia's eyes, a thousand lights that made her whole face shimmer, that pushed his own thoughts of his day from his mind completely. 'Fine.' He brushed it aside as though it meant nothing. 'Yours?'

'Actually, it was pretty wonderful.'

His gut rolled. 'Oh?'

A waiter appeared to take their drinks order. Olivia met his gaze, smiled, and in halting Italian proceeded to order the bottle of Prosecco she enjoyed so much.

'Bene, signorina.' The waiter's eyes lit up.

Luca resisted the impulse to inform the waiter that Olivia was, in fact, a *signora*. What did it matter? She was his wife, they both knew it; nothing else mattered.

He focused his attention back on her face. 'You were saying?'

'My day.' She nodded, pleating her napkin into her lap, searching for the right words. 'I went sightseeing, and I had a revelation.' She paused, and before he could prompt her to continue, the over-zealous, over-attentive waiter appeared, brandishing the Prosecco for *'signorina'*, asking in slow Italian if she would like to taste the bottle. She turned to Luca, lost, and he shook his head, delighting in taking over the conversation.

Was he seriously jealous of a waiter she didn't even know?

He blamed his naturally possessive instincts. It wasn't Olivia he was asserting a claim over, so much as their temporary, meaningless relationship.

'The bottle will suffice,' he said in his native tongue. 'Leave it; I can pour.'

The waiter disappeared with a disgruntled expression.

'What did you say to him? He seemed cross.'

Luca flattened his lips. 'It's not important. You were saying something about a revelation?'

Her eyes chased the waiter with obvious sympathy, but then she blinked back to him, watching as Luca poured a generous measure of bubbles into her flute.

'I didn't go to university, you know. I couldn't have left home. Mum depended on me, and there was too much to do anyway. We couldn't afford any help, and the house was massive.' She pulled her lips to the side, her expression one of timelessness, as though she were back in the past. 'And somewhere along the way, I suppose I've lost sight of—'

The waiter reappeared, notepad in one hand, and a pen in the other.

Luca cursed under his breath. 'Bring us whatever the chef recommends,' he bit out curtly, then, as an afterthought, to Olivia, 'Is that okay?'

Olivia looked bemused. 'Yes. I'm sure that will be fine.' She turned a megawatt smile on the waiter, and, as a result, he left somewhat mollified compared to his previous retreat.

'You're cranky.'

'I've never known a waiter to interrupt so often.'

Her eyes widened with surprise. 'I'm fairly sure that's an ordinary amount, actually.'

'It doesn't matter. You were saying?'

'Yes.' She nodded slowly, then laughed. 'What exactly was I saying?'

'Somewhere along the way, you've lost sight of something.'

'Right.' She sipped her Prosecco, closing her eyes for a brief moment, to savour the ice-cold explosion of flavour. 'I have no idea who I am.'

She delivered the words with complete calm, but there was a tempest in her pale blue eyes, so he knew what a momentous pronouncement that was. 'I don't even remember what I used to want to do with my life, before my father died and everything changed. I suppose the sorts of things every child fantasises about—to become a ballerina, an astronaut, prime minister.' She wrinkled her nose and, out of nowhere, he felt as if he'd been punched, hard. He leaned closer without realising it. 'But then, as a teenager, I never really developed any other goals. I suppose I knew it would be fruitless, that I'd never be free to pursue them. I didn't plan to go to university, I simply accepted that it wouldn't be my fate. And then today, I went to Il Vaticano, and as I toured the rooms, one by one, I remembered something I buried a long, long time ago.'

He leaned forward slightly. 'Which is?'

'I love art. As a child, I used to relish creating paintings, sculptures out of clay, craft from the garden. I adored the ancient paintings that adorned the walls of Hughenwood House, many of which we've had to lease to cover the running costs,' she said with a grimace of regret. 'But it wasn't until today that it occurred to me I could actually pursue art as a career. Or *any* kind of career. Once we divorce, I'll be free for the first time in my adult life. There'll be money to go towards the maintenance of the house, even to restore it to its former glory. I can take a flat in London and go to university, albeit as a mature age student. I can have a real life, Luca.'

His frown was instinctive. 'You do not need to wait until we are divorced—'

'I know,' she interrupted, taking another sip of her drink, her enthusiasm almost as effervescent as the drink. 'I was thinking that, too. And so I decided I'd go to the Vatican every day while you're at the office, and see every bit of art, taking notes on what I like and don't like, then expand to other galleries. I'm in one of the art hubs of the world—what a place to discover myself, and work out exactly what it is I want to do with my life.'

As she spoke, her cheeks grew pink and the sparkle in her eyes took on a stellar quality.

'You're right.' He reached for his own drink, holding the stem in his hands, watching as the bubbles fizzed.

'Anyway, the point is, I'm excited. It's like I'm just realising the horizons that are opening up for me, and it's all thanks to you.'

'Not thanks to me,' he said with a shake of his head.

'Without this marriage, none of it would be possible.'

His brow furrowed as he contemplated her father's will, the barbaric terms that had seen her penalised, infantilised, punished, for no reason other than her gender.

'A regrettable circumstance.'

She tilted her head to the side, studying him for a moment before a shy smile spread over her lips. 'I don't regret it though, Luca. I really don't.'

Strangely, nor did Luca.

CHAPTER TEN

LUCA PICKED UP his phone with the totally foreign sensation that he was floating on air, calling Olivia without a moment's thought. She answered on the third ring.

'How's *il Papa* today?'

'I haven't seen him, yet,' she responded, quick as a whip. 'But if I do, I'll tell him you said hi.'

'Careful, he probably thinks I dance with the devil as much as the rest of Italy does.'

'Then I'll disabuse him of that mistaken belief, and tell him that you're actually a bit of a guardian angel.'

What was that grinding sensation in the pit of his stomach? 'Hardly,' he demurred, but a smile crossed his face.

'Are you home?' Her simple question took on a breathy quality.

'No.' He flicked a glance at his Montblanc

watch. 'I'm calling to see if you can join me for a thing tonight.'

'A "thing"?' she repeated with obvious amusement.

'My offer for Azzuri Bank has been formally accepted by the board. The announcement went out this morning, and to celebrate the news, and encourage a smooth transition, the previous owners and I will be hosting a party this evening. It's going to be quite an event—high profile, lots of celebrities and, therefore, lots of paparazzi.'

'And it would be helpful for you to have a wife on hand?' she murmured. Was that strain in her voice? He wished he weren't so attuned to her, so aware of her every mood.

'Frankly, yes.'

She was quiet for a beat too long, but when she spoke, her voice was light-hearted enough. But was it sincere? Or forced, for his sake? 'Then of course I'll come. Where?'

'I'll pick you up from home.' He didn't give it a second thought, relief whooshing through him. 'Can you be ready by eight?'

The amusement crept back into her words. 'It's two o'clock. How long do you think I'll need?'

'About thirty-seven seconds,' he agreed. 'You could pull on a hessian sack and outshine anyone else in attendance.'

The throwaway remark seemed to spark something in Olivia though. 'Hmm, but there will be a heap of people, right?'

'About two hundred.'

She let out a low whistle. 'And you said celebrities?'

'*Sì*. Clients of the bank—old Italian money, celebrities, you know the sort.'

'So the dress code is—what?'

'Conservative black tie.'

'A ball gown?'

'A dress of some sort,' he responded. 'Ideally something that will not be too complicated to remove as soon as we are home again.'

Olivia was quiet, and he hated that he couldn't see her face, because he had no idea what that silence represented. She didn't laugh at his quip.

'Okay, I'll see you at eight.'

A Cinderella moment might have been a fantasy for many women but, for Olivia, the longer she spent being transformed into a society wife, the more ice flooded her veins, until eventually, a little before eight that night, she met her reflection with sheer trepidation. Look back at her from the full-length mirror in the bedroom was a younger version of her mother.

She'd turned into what she'd always run from, what she'd been made to run from. At first, she'd planned to do her own hair and make-up, but it wasn't as though she had much experience with either, so on a whim she'd asked Signora Marazzi to book her into a salon. The chic stylist assigned to her had spoken enough English to understand what Olivia had wanted, but somehow the instructions for 'understated' had still resulted in, frankly, a work of art. It was to the stylist's credit, not Olivia's, that her face was exquisitely made up. She wore barely any foundation—*'Because your skin is so glowing, we not want to cover it, eh?'* But her eyes had been made to look like a tiger's, with delicate eyeliner slashing out at the corner, and mascara applied liberally to her naturally long lashes, so she felt as though she were a film star from the sixties. A hint of bronzer on her cheeks, and cherry red on her lips, a complete diversion from her usual, natural colour. Her blonde hair had been styled into voluptuous curls and pinned over one shoulder, the perfect complement to the dress she wore—one of the gowns that he'd given her in Venice.

Their honeymoon hadn't been that long ago, and yet, she felt as though she were a different person. Luca was so new to her then, so unknown. So much had changed—between them, and within her. She was now an entirely different person, almost unrecognisable to herself.

When she'd tried on the gown—a silk slip dress that fell to the floor, with delicate ribbons for sleeves and a neckline that revealed just a hint of cleavage, in a colour that was silver, like wet sand in the moonlight—she had wondered if she'd ever wear it. It made a little too much of her assets, showing off her rounded breasts, her neat waist and gently swollen hips, her rounded bottom. She hadn't thought she'd *ever* want to draw attention to herself, the kind of attention a dress like this demanded. And she still didn't want attention. At least, not from the crowds, not from random strangers. But from her husband?

Heat took over the ice in her body as she imagined Luca's response to the dress. For him, this was worth it.

She slid her feet into heels, the red soles just visible as she walked, grabbed a clutch purse from her dressing table and checked it for the essentials—phone, credit card, lipstick—then made her way to the top of the stairs. Purely by happenstance, the front door opened as she reached the landing, so she had a moment to observe Luca without his knowledge. He'd changed at the office, into a jet-black tuxedo and snowy white shirt, a black bow tie at his neck. It was a completely appropriate outfit and yet his primal, raw energy made a mockery of the formality of his tuxedo. Even the suit couldn't hide the fact that he had a latent energy just waiting to be expelled. Her heart leaped in instant recognition, moving from its position in her chest and somehow taking up almost all the space within her body, so its rapid beating was all she was conscious of.

She placed her hand on the railing to steady herself, her wedding ring glinting in the evening light. She stared at it for a moment—for courage?—then began to move down the stairs.

Since when had her wedding ring become an object of strength? Initially she'd viewed it as a mark of possession, something she'd resented almost as much as the necessity of this marriage, and now she took comfort from it? Olivia didn't want to analyse that—she could barely acknowledge it to herself—as though she knew danger lurked somewhere behind the realisation, a danger she didn't want to face.

Luca placed his wallet and phone on the hall stand when a slight movement caught his eye and he turned, chasing it down before anticipating that it might be Olivia. One look at her and the world stopped spinning, all the breath in his body burst from him, and his eyes seemed incapable of leaving her.

She was—there was no way to describe her. 'Beautiful' was a word he'd used before, to describe other women at other times, so there was no way he could apply it to Olivia now, because she was more magnificent, breathtaking and overwhelmingly stunning than he'd ever known a woman could be. Her eyes held his as she moved down the stairs, and with each step she took it was as though an invisible cord formed between them, knotting, putting them together inexorably, unavoidably, until she reached the bottom of the stairs and then they were both moving, his strides long and determined to her elegant.

They stopped a few feet apart. *He* stopped, because he wanted to be able to see her properly, and she stopped because she hesitated. Her eyes clouded with something like uncertainty. As though she sought reassurance. Surely not. Olivia had to know that she was the most spectacular woman who'd ever walked the earth.

'What do you think?' she asked after a moment, her eyes almost pleading with him to reassure her.

A frown pulled at Luca's mouth. What was he missing? Her hand lifted, self-consciously running over her hair, and he remembered her disclosure about the time she'd applied make-up and done her hair, for her twelfth birthday party, and her mother had overreacted. She'd never dressed up again.

Not until now.

His gut twisted at his insensitivity, at the momentousness of this night, and he ached to reassure her and comfort her, but his own body was still in a sense of shock at the sight of Olivia, so it took him a few moments longer than he would have liked.

'I wasn't sure if it was appropriate.' She dug her teeth into her perfect, bright red lower lip and every part of him tightened. He wanted to cancel the whole damned night. He wanted to throw her over his shoulder and take her back upstairs to bed, to strip the dress from her body and destroy her perfectly curled hair, to run his fingers through it until the curls were untidy and her make-up was smudged from passion. He wanted…but that was precisely the lack of control he wouldn't allow into this marriage. It was the reason he'd been forcing himself to stick to his regular work schedule, to limit their time together. It would be so easy to forget the terms of their marriage, to allow himself to want *more* of Olivia, and he would never put himself in that position again. He established the boundaries of his life. He relied on no one. He loved *no one.* Jayne had taught him well there, and it was a lesson he never intended to forget.

'You are perfect,' he said, the word coming to him out of nowhere. But it was the right way to describe her. He reached out, running the back of his hand over her hair. She swept her eyes shut, impossibly long lashes forming half-crescents against her cheeks.

'Not too much?'

'Perfect,' he said again.

'I wasn't sure.'

Her insecurity made him simultaneously sorry for her and furious on her behalf. How

could a twenty-four-year-old woman be so un-
sure of herself? Her mother had failed Olivia
completely. She'd been denied all opportunities to experiment socially and to explore herself, so that she might know who and what she
was. And yet, somehow, Olivia had come out
of it as socially adept and fascinating as anyone he'd ever known. It was only her looks that
made Olivia uncomfortable, as though by dressing to attract attention she was stepping into an
unknown arena, one she'd prefer not to occupy.

'You will be the most beautiful woman in
the room tonight.' *And every night*, he silently
added.

Ambivalence flared inside Olivia. There was
pleasure at his praise, his obvious admiration, but there was also a deep sense of guilt,
as though she were betraying her mother. She
offered a tight smile, then looked to the door.
'Should we go?'

His eyes held hers for a beat too long. '*Sì.* And
we will stay only as long as is absolutely necessary.'

There was promise in those words and it fired
heat deep within her, pushing everything else
aside.

Olivia was aware of Luca on a cell-deep level in every minute that passed, from the moment they exited the house until they arrived at a restaurant across from the gold-lit Coliseum, the ancient stadium taking Olivia's breath away for a moment. She wasn't aware of the photographers standing in a roped-off area to the side of the doors—she was, briefly, not even fully aware of Luca, as she stood and gaped at the sight, surrounded by the hum of evening traffic, so stately and terrific, her heart trembling as she imagined the scenes of terror that had been played out, while simultaneously admiring the craftsmanship of creating such an epic space.

'Have you ever toured it?' His breath fanned her cheek, bringing her back to the moment with a rush.

She shook her head. 'We didn't have time when I came as a child.'

'And this week you have been far too busy with the Pope,' Luca teased, reaching down and weaving their fingers together. It was such a natural gesture, Olivia had to remind herself it was all completely for show.

'That's right. Though perhaps next week,' she said, and then, with a small frown furrowing her brows, 'Definitely before I leave Rome.'

It was like the setting of a stopwatch, or perhaps simply reminding them of the incessant ticking of time in the background of their lives.

They were halfway into this marriage of theirs. Two weeks down, two weeks to go. She glanced up at him but his expression gave nothing away.

Whatever she'd been about to say flew from her mind as a photographer's bulb flashed close by and instinctively Olivia flinched closer to Luca.

'Smile through it,' he advised, squeezing her hand as they began to walk towards the doors. Questions were flung at him as they went, in Italian, so she could only pick out certain words. Corporate. Purchase. Record-breaking. Scandal. Tradition. Outcry.

It was enough to draw her gaze to his face once more, but he was implacable, as though he hadn't heard a single question.

They moved through the doors, into a restaurant that was far more charming than Olivia had expected. The tables and chairs she imagined usually filled the restaurant had been removed, leaving only a tiled floor covered in the expensive shoes of Italy's wealthiest personalities. She recognised very few of those in attendance and was glad—there were none of the nerves one might have felt when rubbing shoulders with celebrities you knew and admired.

'The usual.' But his voice was gruff, sparking questions inside her.

'Is there a scandal because you've bought the bank?'

'They are alluding to the scandal of my past.'

'Your father's scandal?'

'Italian society has a long memory,' he said with a smile that didn't reach his eyes. 'Let us find you a drink.'

The first hour passed in a whir of introductions, and, despite the fact Luca insisted on speaking English for Olivia's benefit, conversation switched back and forth, from Italian to English, at breakneck speed, so she found it almost impossible to keep up. He didn't leave her side, nor did he drop her hand, so despite the fact she felt completely off the deep end, she was also enjoying herself, the spectacle, the vibe, the noise, the joy of life. It was the sort of event she'd never attended—something she'd read about online or seen in movies, but to actually attend, and with the star of the show, was actually surprisingly fun. When the room was so full she could barely move, he turned to her.

'I have to make a speech.' He pressed a kiss to the soft flesh just beneath her ear, sending a thousand sparks into her bloodstream. 'It will be in Italian, but you'll get the gist. Excuse me.'

Olivia watched as he made his way through the crowd, his dark head inches above most, his shoulders broad, his stride somehow cutting through the gathering of people with ease.

At the front of the restaurant, a microphone had been set up, and even before Luca approached it, the crowd grew quiet.

When he spoke, it was as though Olivia were being pressed back against a wall. She saw him as he appeared to the rest of the world, as he'd appeared to her, the first time they'd met. He was no longer Luca, the man she'd come to know so well, but a powerful, self-made tycoon with more strength, arrogance and ambition than anyone that had ever lived. The crowd was completely captivated by him, the effect of his words inspiring laughter, then nods of agreement.

She was in awe.

'You are here with Luca?' The question was unwelcome, an intrusion on a private moment between Olivia and Luca—despite the fact hundreds of people surrounded them. She blinked away from him, annoyed, meeting the eyes of a beautiful dark-haired woman.

'Yes.' She smiled crisply then turned back to her husband.

'I wondered why I had not heard from him. Have you been together long?'

'Only a couple of weeks,' Olivia said, before remembering they were supposed to be playing the part of a happily married couple.

'Then I'm sure it's almost at an end. He never strays for long.'

Hairs on the back of Olivia's neck stood on end. 'Oh?' The other woman smiled banally, but her claws were out. Olivia felt them trying to find purchase in her back.

'He will get bored of you soon enough, and then he'll be back in my bed.'

Olivia's heart slammed into her ribs. This vile, beautiful woman was right. When their marriage ended, Luca would return to his normal life, and resume his normal activities, which, Olivia gathered, included this woman. It was the expectation Olivia had come into this marriage with, and nothing had changed to affect that. So why did her throat now feel filled with sawdust?

'Perhaps.' Olivia tilted her head to the side,

affecting a look of nonchalance. If there was one thing she was glad of, it was that her up-bringing had equipped her with all the skills to hide how she was feeling. To an onlooker, she appeared as zen as one could get. 'That's really up to Luca.'

The reply surprised the other woman, taking the wind out of her sails completely. She left without another word. But all of the enjoyment of the night had faded for Olivia, and she couldn't say precisely why. After all, nothing had changed. She'd married Luca knowing it was fake, and temporary. They had agreed to sleep together on the basis that sex wouldn't change the cold terms of their marriage. He would go back to his life, as it had been before her, and that shouldn't bother her. So why did it? Why did Olivia suddenly feel as though she were falling into the depths of the ocean? Why did it feel as though she were drowning?

'You are very quiet.'

Olivia blinked up at Luca, annoyed at herself for not having been able to fool him into thinking everything was fine. After all, it was fine, wasn't it?

'Perhaps I'm tired,' she offered.

Luca's eyes skimmed the room. The crowd had thinned a little, but, at almost midnight, the party was still in full swing, the voices growing louder as the alcohol intake grew.

'We'll leave.'

'We don't have to,' she demurred with a shake of her head.

He leaned closer, breathing into her ear. 'I want to. We've stayed far longer than I intended. Let's go home.'

It was such a simple, oft-repeated phrase. It meant nothing. But when Luca referred to 'home', a hole formed right in the middle of Olivia's heart, because his wonderful property in the heart of Rome was not, and never would be, her home. That was in England, the dreaded Hughenwood House, and soon Olivia would have to return there. Not for long, but initially, to sort out their business affairs and launch herself into a new life. Uncertainty made her stomach off-kilter. It was the future she'd longed for, the future she'd fought damned hard for, even marrying a total stranger to achieve, so why did it stand before her like a pit of lava she was now obliged to cross?

CHAPTER ELEVEN

'DID YOU ENJOY yourself last night?'

Olivia flipped her face on the pillows, eyeing Luca with a sardonic expression. 'Are you taking a victory lap, Signor Giovanardi?'

He frowned.

'I should have thought my enjoyment—on multiple occasions—was self-evident.'

He roared with laughter, lifting a hand and pressing it to his forehead. 'That is, naturally, very gratifying, but actually, I was asking about the party.'

'Oh.'

He will get bored of you soon enough.

She covered the glut of displeasure and the strange taste that filled her mouth with a steady smile. She hadn't been able to push the other woman from her mind, not for long, anyway.

'It was…fascinating.'

He grinned, lifting onto one elbow and regarding her thoughtfully. 'Fascinating? What exactly does this mean?'

'Oh, just unlike anything I've ever experienced.'

'Surely you've been to parties?'

She studied the ceiling, lost in thought. 'Not a lot, actually. As a teenager, a few casual things, but after that, not really.'

'You really have lived the life of a recluse.'

'Yes.'

'And after this?'

She turned to look at him, then wished she hadn't. Her heart clutched, echoing the worst indigestion she'd ever known. She'd been trying so hard not to think about 'after'. Why did he have to bring it up? 'What do you mean?'

'What will your life be like?'

She really didn't want to think about it. 'I don't know.' She inched closer, her body craving him despite the hours they'd spent exploring one another the night before. In the back of her brain, she imagined nights without Luca, and wondered how she'd cope, how her body would cope, without him.

'Is this normal?' She blurted the question out before she could second-guess the wisdom of asking him something so telling.

'Our life here?'

Our life. Pain sheared her chest. She blinked away, focusing beyond him. 'No, I mean...' She swallowed past a lump of embarrassment.

'Sì?'

'Erm...sex. The way it is with us...is it always like this?'

He reached out, pressing a finger to her chin, drawing her gaze back to his face. 'No.'

Something shifted inside her. She bit down on her lower lip.

'At least, not in my experience.'

'How is it different?'

'Now who's taking a victory lap?'

'Is that what I'm doing?' she murmured. 'I wouldn't know. I have zero experience.'

'That's true.' He moved closer, so their hips met, his arousal pressing to her, and fierce heat flashed in her body.

'He bores easily.'

The question shaped in her mouth, but she found it almost impossible to ask. Shyness stole through her, even as they lay together, naked, far from strangers, so she couldn't simply ask him about the other woman, about what their relationship was. Or was it that Olivia didn't want to hear the answer? Was it that she couldn't bear to hear the answer? And if so, why was that? Where was the cold dispassion she'd been banking on? When was the last time she'd been with Luca and not felt as though a part of her were burning alive? And why did she suddenly want to grab hold of him with both hands and never let go?

Stricken, she could only stare at him, as her brain kept throwing questions at her, forcing her to face reality, to answer them, to acknowledge that what was supposed to be a straightforward marriage agreement was suddenly so much more complex.

A buzzing pierced the room, so Olivia glanced at Luca's bedside table first, where his phone sat with a dark screen, then over her shoulder to her own bedside table. Her sister's face filled the front of the device. She reached for it gratefully. Saved by the bell.

'It's Sienna,' she said crisply. 'If it were anyone else, I'd leave it…'

His eyes sparked as though filing away that piece of information, but Olivia was already rolling away, disappointment curdling inside of her at the distance between them.

'Hey, Sisi.'

'Libby! What the heck is going on?'

Familiarity was a new kind of warmth, running over Olivia, at the sound of her childhood nickname. 'What do you mean?'

'Are you actually engaged to Luca Giovanardi?'

Olivia sat upright, her eyes bolting to Luca's. 'Why do you ask?'

'Because it's in the papers. Mum's beside herself, which, I have to say, is actually kind of funny, but then, you did look ridiculously beautiful in the photos and you know she hates that.'

'What photos?'

'Have you not been online today?'

'No, I—' She glanced at the time and pulled a face. It was later than she'd realised. 'Haven't had a chance.'

'Well, there are enough gossip pieces about you and Luca Giovanardi to keep you busy a while. Speculation that you're engaged—even married.' Sienna's voice lowered to a hushed, earnest tone. 'I know about dad's stupid will, Libby. You really did it, didn't you?'

What else could I have done? She didn't ask it, because the answer was simple. Leave them living in destitution. Leave her mother paying the price of her father's cruelty for the rest of her life? Or worst of all, leave it to Sienna to get married before the deadline and improve their fortunes? None of those options were possible. This marriage was all Olivia could do, and yet she didn't resent it. She sure as hell didn't regret it.

'What else are the papers saying?'

'Let me see.' Olivia could imagine Sienna clicking open her iPad. 'There's a ton of pictures, all very nice. A bit of background on Luca, some scandal with his father a long time ago, his very, very varied dating past, including photos of—phwoar, did you know he used to date Elizabeth Mason?'

Olivia tried not to conjure images of the stunning American actress—and failed, so all she could see was Luca and Elizabeth, and what a beautiful pair they'd make. Jealousy gripped her, hard.

'There's a close-up of your hand—nice ring, by the way. And— Oh. This is a new article.'

Olivia tensed. 'What is it?'

"In response to fierce speculation that one of Italy's most eligible bachelors has been removed from the market for good, Luca Giovanardi's grandmother Pietra has released a short statement confirming the marriage. 'My grandson has finally found happiness, and with

a woman who is quite his perfect match. I am very pleased for them both.""'

All the air whooshed out of Olivia.

'You *are* married?' Sienna squeaked. 'Tell me this isn't true?'

Olivia scrunched up her face, aware that Luca was watching her intently. 'It's true.'

'Oh, Libby. Darling, you didn't have to do this.'

'Didn't I?' She turned to face Luca and her heart jolted in her chest. *Didn't I?*

He reached out, putting his hand on her knee, a question in his eyes. She looked away. Questions were all she could feel now, questions about her choices, her feelings, and, most importantly, her desires. Because knowing their marriage was coming to an end felt like the slow dropping of an executioner's blade, and she desperately wanted to slow it, or to stop it altogether. She could barely breathe.

'No! This is for the money, isn't it? Oh, Libby. Why didn't you talk to me about this? We could have worked something out.'

Olivia compressed her lips. She'd shielded Sienna from the worst of their financial situation, protecting her sister from the truth of just how bad things had been for them, but the truth was they'd have been ruined if she hadn't gone through with this.

'Let's discuss it when I'm home.'

'And when will that be?'

'Two weeks. A little less.' Her heart splintered, her lungs burned.

'And will your *husband* be coming?' She layered the word with cynical disapproval and the bite of disapproval from kind-hearted Sienna hurt like hell—almost as much as the realisation that Luca wouldn't be joining her on that trip, or any other, once their brief arranged marriage was at an end.

'No. I'll come alone.' Her voice cracked a little. She swallowed to clear the hoarse feeling in her throat. 'I'll talk to you later, Sisi.'

She disconnected the call and pasted a determinedly bright smile on her face. 'Well, that went about as well as could be expected.'

'You didn't tell her about any of this?'

'No.'

'Why not?'

'Because I didn't think she would approve, and if anyone can talk me out of anything, it's my sister.'

Olivia placed the phone down and stared straight ahead, at the wall across the room.

'And were you right? Does she not approve?'

'It doesn't sound like it.' She pleated the sheet between her forefinger and thumb. 'Sienna is the kindest person you'll ever meet, but I've tried very hard to keep her from understanding the ins and outs of our family's financial predicament.'

'So you alone have borne this worry?'

Olivia tilted him a steady look. 'I'm the oldest.'

Disapproval marred his features. 'Your parents have failed you.'

She pulled a face. 'Look who's talking.'

'Perhaps that's why I can recognise the signs so easily.' He reached out, drawing her down to him then bringing his body over hers. 'You deserved so much better, Olivia.'

Their eyes met and understanding passed between them, a fierce sense of agreement, and then his head lowered, his mouth seeking hers, gently at first, as if to reassure her through his kiss, and then with urgency, passion overtaking them. Already naked, he simply pushed aside the sheet between them, and drove into her, so Olivia cried out with pleasure at his immediate, urgent possession, his arousal filling her, moving fast, deep, his rhythm demanding, explicit, exactly what she needed.

'It is not always like this,' he promised against her mouth, reminding her of their earlier conversation. 'I find I cannot get enough of you.'

Pleasure curled through her as his words mixed with the physical sensations he was arousing with such need, until she was incandescent with heat and fever, building to an unavoidable release, perfectly coinciding with his own explosion.

'I can't get enough of you either,' she admitted, when their breathing had slowed and he'd rolled onto his back, bringing her with him, so her head lay on his chest. His heart thumped heavily beneath her. *I can't get enough of you, but, eventually, this will have to be enough.* Their marriage would come to an end, and, while she was regretting that, there was a part of Olivia that was also glad. There was a danger here she hadn't appreciated at first, a danger of wanting so much more from Luca than she'd originally anticipated—and he was just the kind of man who would swallow her whole.

Olivia knew that love was a very dangerous force, and she'd always sworn she would avoid it, rather than turn into the kind of woman her mother had become, in the service of love. She just hadn't appreciated that love was a force all of its own, that it could chase after you when you had no intention of being caught, that it could bombard you and threaten to wrap around you unless you were ever, ever vigilant. And being vigilant while in the arms and bed of Luca Giovanardi was proving almost impossible.

Soon, it would be over, and she'd be able to breathe again. Wouldn't she?

'My grandmother has asked us to visit her for a night or two. Do you have any objections?'

Olivia met Luca's questioning gaze as she stepped out of the shower. He stood draped against the bathroom door jamb, his presence not an invasion so much as a sign of the intimacy she'd begun to accept as totally normal. In the back of her mind, a warning bell was almost constantly sounding, the small incursions something she knew she should fight back against. After all, she'd always sworn she'd maintain her independence and autonomy, but with Luca all her barriers were being eroded—and she didn't seem to mind. But there was no threat here. No danger. They knew when and how their relationship would end. She would never turn into her mother, no matter how much she surrendered to him, and this.

Ever-hungry, her gaze feasted upon his physique, her mouth drying as it always did when she allowed herself to drool.

'Olivia? Eyes up here.'

Guilt flushed her cheeks. 'Of course not. It's one of the main reasons we married.' She answered his question with a hint of embarrassment at having been caught out. But he laughed and prowled towards her, whipping the towel from her body.

'My turn.' He stepped back, and his own inspection of her was so much slower, his gaze travelling from the tip of her head to her toes and back again, lingering on her curves, her most intimate body parts, until her breath was coming in pants.

'Luca.' The word burst from her.

'I know.' His eyes flashed with an emotion she didn't understand and then he drew her into his arms, kissing her soundly. A kiss was never enough, though. It was the flicking of a switch, the lighting of a torch that had to be burned down completely before it could be released. She kissed him back with full comprehension of that, her body cleaved to his, naked, hungry, yearning, as his hands reached behind her back and pressed her to him. She ground her hips to him, and heard the sharp expulsion of air, and then he was pulling apart, fire in his eyes as he glared down at her, heat in his cheeks.

He dropped to his knees and she groaned, because at first she thought he was ending what they shared, but then he separated her legs and brought his mouth to her sex, kissing her and whipping her into a frenzy, so she had to brace her palms on the marble counter, head tilted backwards, vaguely aware of what a wanton sight she must make—and not giving even half a damn. How could she care about anything but pleasure when there was pleasure such as this?

'Signora Giovanardi, thank you for coming.'

'My husband's message said it was important?'

The assistant nodded. 'Signor Giovanardi is just concluding a meeting and has asked you to wait in his office. This way, please.' The deference with which Olivia's assistants treated her brought a smile to Olivia's lips, but she was aware, all the time, of how temporary this was. When she wanted to savour every moment of their marriage, instead it was rushing towards its conclusion, seconds passing in a blur, days flicking by, so that she knew there was barely any time left.

She fell into step beside the receptionist, and, at the door to Luca's office, dredged up something like a smile. 'Thank you.'

'Would you like anything to drink? Tea? Coffee? Wine?'

Olivia suppressed a smile at the Italian indulgence for a lunchtime *aperitivo*. 'A mineral water would be lovely, thank you. It's warm out there today.'

'Indeed. Summers in Rome are unbearably humid.'

Olivia thought of the dark, dank hall at Hughenwood House, contrasting it to the sun-filled streets she'd traversed on the walk to Luca's office. 'I think it's lovely,' she murmured as the assistant left the room.

When she was alone, curiosity got the better of her, and she wandered towards his desk first, admiring the spotless work environment. No clutter, no personal effects, no photographs, just a laptop, and a Manilla folder with the word 'Singapore' on the side. She ran a finger over the top then eyed the boardroom table. Several more folders sat here. She moved to them out of idle curiosity and pulled up short when she saw her name on the side of one.

THORNTON-ROSE

Another folder, beside it.

HUGHENWOOD HOUSE

And another.

PORTFOLIO

Heart thumping, she was torn. It was abundantly obvious that these folders pertained to her, and her business, and yet she felt like a snoop to open them and look inside. Torn, she prevaricated and a moment later the door opened. She looked up, expecting to see his assistant, only to be met by the appearance of Luca, striding in with sheer, obvious impatience, his shirt unbuttoned at the collar, his hair tousled as though he'd been driving his fingers through it all morning.

He stopped short when their eyes met, a grim line on his lips before he changed direction and closed the distance. The door opened once more, and the receptionist followed with a tray—two coffees, a bottle of mineral water, and a plate of biscotti.

'Thank you,' Luca dismissed, without looking in his assistant's direction.

Once they were alone again, he lifted a coffee cup and extended it to Olivia. Their fingers brushed and sparks shot through her, sparks she might have imagined would have faded by now, but which had, instead, intensified, overtaking her completely. She took the coffee on autopilot, staring at the golden liquid a moment. She hadn't wanted a coffee, but now that it was in her hands, she took a sip, relishing the strong, bitter flavour.

'You left a message for me to meet you here,' Olivia reminded him, wondering at the strange sense of hesitation—an emotion she hadn't felt a moment ago. But seeing the folders had unsettled her—it was as if her old life was slipping into the room with them, reminding her forcibly of why they'd married. It was a reminder she resented.

'Yes.' He looked awkward. Her heart went into overdrive. Was she here to discuss their marriage? They still had a little over a week left. Surely they didn't have to talk about the end just yet? She knew she was living in a fantasy land but Olivia wasn't ready to face the practicalities of leaving him—yet. When the time came, she would. She'd be strong, just as she had been at every other time in her life where strength was required, but for the moment she wanted to blot out the path ahead. Unless…what if he wanted to change the terms of their agreement? What if he wanted to extend things? Hope was an unstoppable force, exploding in her chest. She dug her fingernails into her palms, waiting, wishing, wondering…

'I'd like to discuss your finances,' he said with quiet control. 'Or rather, their ongoing management.'

Olivia could have been knocked over with a feather. 'Oh.' *Was that all?*

'I'm sorry to say, yet not surprised, I admit, that the lawyers handling your father's estate are as misogynistic as he evidently was. I was contacted earlier in the week and advised that I could collect this information on your behalf, now that we are legally married.'

'They've been ignoring my calls,' she said with a sigh.

'Bastards.'

'You're angry?'

'Aren't you?'

'Well, yes, of course.'

'I cannot see any God-given reason you should require your husband to collect your own financial documents,' he responded curtly, his anger obviously not directed at her.

Olivia's heart skipped a beat. His support was something she hadn't known she needed.

'I know financial independence is your goal and I'm sorry I've had to be involved in obtaining this information—however, these files contain everything you'll need to know about your family's business affairs. The money that is now yours, how it is invested, as well as other investments that will pass to you.'

Olivia blinked, her stomach twisting.

'There is also information pertaining to your sister's inheritance.'

'Thank you.'

His eyes narrowed, darkening. 'Don't thank me, Olivia. You should never have needed me, for any of this.'

Her heart swelled. 'But it's not your fault that I did. And I am grateful to you, Luca.'

His mood didn't improve and warmth spread through her. It was a sign of his decency and loyalty that he was so incensed.

'Please, have a look.' He gestured to the files.

'I will be working over here, and am happy to answer any questions you have. Alternatively, I have the name of an excellent financial advisor, and can put you in touch. Just let me know.'

He nodded curtly, all business, so she wanted to start removing her clothing, piece by piece, to jolt him back to the intimacy they shared, the heat that exploded between them. And yet, how could she overlook this gesture? He was making everything as easy as possible for her. Right down to offering help without presuming she'd need it. He wasn't mansplaining things to her, but rather allowing her to find her own feet, waiting until she asked for assistance, but letting her know it would be freely given. It was the perfect gesture, and she was touched, right to the centre of her core; even, she feared, to the centre of her heart.

CHAPTER TWELVE

'HOW COME YOU didn't tell me?'

He paused, carrying her holdall over one shoulder as though it weighed nothing. 'Tell you what?'

Olivia wrinkled her nose. 'Well, that this place would be so—'

They looked around the entrance with its turquoise walls just visible behind dozens of paintings, each showing a different landscape or still life. The floor was large, marble tiles, and in the centre of the ceiling, a chandelier hung, ornate and—Olivia guessed—original to the history of the house. The exterior walls were a washed pink, and the garden was every bit as bright as the home suggested—exotic splashes of colour every which way.

'Extra? Over the top? Garish?'

'Perfect,' Olivia said on a sigh.

'I knew I liked you.' Nonna appeared from behind them, unseen and unannounced, her slender frame elegant in black trousers and a lemon-yellow blouse. Her hair was coiffed into a bun, high on her head, and a daisy pin that sparkled with, Olivia presumed, real diamonds gave the hairstyle some fun and glamour. 'Don't pay my grandson any attention. He's all about bland, modern aesthetic, whereas I prefer—' She swept a manicured hand around the entrance.

'Psychedelic vomit?' Luca drawled with a grin, so Olivia suspected this sort of sparring was the norm for them.

'Evidence of a life well lived.' Pietra winked at Olivia then embraced her, kissing both cheeks. 'I'm so happy you could join me. Come, I'll give you a tour.' She fixed Luca with a glare that was mock irritated. '*You* can put the bags in the room.'

He did a navy salute and Olivia couldn't help chuckling to herself as she was led away by Pietra. The entranceway was really just a hint of the bright, joyous décor throughout. Each room boasted a bright colour scheme, cheerful and somehow cohesive. Despite the fact there could be, in some rooms, blue walls and green curtains, there was always an element that drew it together, such as a sofa with matching cushions that picked up the colour scheme across the entire room, so it was far less chaotic and more harmoniously happy.

'It is a beautiful home.' Olivia sighed as they finished the tour on a balcony with black wrought iron and an abundance of red geraniums, which tumbled from their terracotta pots towards the pool below.

'Thank you. I am pleased you like it. In fact, may I make a confession?'

Olivia nodded slowly.

'I was nervous this morning.'

'Nervous?' Olivia's smile spread over her face. 'Whatever for?'

'That you might, perhaps, not like my home. That you might not want to come.' Nonna's eyes sailed across the countryside, fixing on Positano, sprawled beneath them. 'You see, Luca's all I have, and I couldn't bear it if you and I were anything other than friends. There is not so long left for me, and I want to enjoy the time I have—'

Emotions burst through Olivia, chief amongst them grief that none of this was real. Nonna was offering genuine friendship and Olivia knew it would never really come to pass. Her fake marriage was almost over. After this weekend, Olivia was quite sure she and Pietra would never see one another again. She blinked back a rush of tears and focused on saying what Nonna obviously needed to hear.

'I don't think my marriage would survive if I did anything to alienate you. I know how much you mean to Luca.' She couldn't acknowledge the older woman's reference to her mortality.

'And he to me.' Pietra reached out, tapping a hand on Olivia's. 'And you, *carina*. I never thought, after Jayne, that he would allow himself to love. It was such a bad time in his life, such a hard time for him all round, let alone dealing with her awful treatment. He pushed everyone away, even me, for a long time. I honestly believed I was going to lose him.'

Olivia regarded the older woman thoughtfully. 'Was it really so bad?'

'Oh, worse than you can even imagine. Every friend deserted him. My son swindled them all, you see. No, not every friend. There was one—Alejandro—who stuck by Luca. A man worth his weight in gold. But everyone else, including Jayne, turned their backs on him.' She waved a hand in the air, as if to dispel the recollection of such an unhappy time. 'And now, with you, he is happy. He is himself. Thank you.'

Olivia was overwhelmed—with emotions at

the compliment, with guilt because it wasn't real, and then with sadness because she wanted, more than anything, for all of this to be true. The thought struck her like a lightning bolt, but it didn't come completely out of the blue. No, there had been precipitation and storm clouds building for days, suggesting that nothing was as it had first appeared, that everything had changed since their fateful wedding. There was also a jealousy—unmistakable now—for Luca's first wife. A woman he'd once loved, loved enough to have been destroyed by. Loved enough to have sworn off love and relationships evermore.

'And you are happy,' Nonna continued, then winced. 'Or you were, until I started to meddle.'

'Not meddle.' Olivia shook her head. 'I'm just…touched…that you have such faith in us.'

'Who that has seen you together could fail to have faith? And I must believe, you see, because soon I will be gone, and I do not want him to be alone.' Her voice cracked. 'Luca acts so tough, as though he doesn't need anyone, but when I look at my grandson, I still see the little boy I used to bounce on my knee. I want the best for him, *carina*.' Nonna's voice was a little wobbly and she pulled away with a determined effort to laugh. 'But enough of this. I am being too maudlin; Luca would not approve.' She straightened, making an obvious attempt to appear relaxed. 'You must go and explore the town while it is daylight.' She waved a hand towards the exceptional view of Positano. 'Dinner is served at six—I am afraid I eat unfashionably early these days; my medication makes me tired.' Before Olivia could offer a comment of condolence, Pietra pushed on, 'But it leaves you free to do something wonderful tonight, afterwards, no?'

Positano defied every single one of Olivia's expectations. It was prettier than a postcard, with the buildings carved into the cliff-face, a tumbling mix of colourful houses, terracotta roofs and the backdrop of greenery that grew beyond it. She walked beside Luca as he traced the well-worn path he'd traipsed as a child and teenager, pointing out interesting titbits as they went, until finally they began to descend, steep steps carrying them towards the beach and the busy main street that ran parallel to it. Cafes spilled out with tables and umbrellas playing host to a mix of elegant locals and happy, loud tourists. The boutiques boasted beautiful clothes and homewares, so Olivia scanned each with growing interest as they walked.

'Hungry?'

She only realised, as he asked the question, that she hadn't eaten all day. Never a big breakfaster, she'd woken with butterflies in her tummy at the prospect of travelling to Nonna's home, and the idea of remaining for an entire weekend. Of course, she shouldn't have worried, and now that she'd met Pietra again, the nerves had abated, and her hunger had returned.

'Actually, yes. Shall we grab something light? Nonna said dinner is served at six.'

He pulled a face so Olivia laughed softly. 'She also said that eating early leaves us free to do something wonderful after dinner...'

His expression relaxed immediately, speculation darkening his eyes. 'She's very clever.' He pulled Olivia against him, kissing her right there in the middle of the street, where tourists milled about them and the sun beat down, warm and golden.

Breathless, Olivia pulled away, something like hope trembling in her mind. This marriage was nothing like they'd planned for. 'Where do you suggest?'

'I know just the place.'

She smiled. 'Of course you do.'

In Positano, Luca was treated like royalty. He

knew many of the shopkeepers, who came out to shake his hand as he passed, and each of the restaurant owners gestured towards tables, inviting them in, but he smiled, offered a kind word, a promise for 'next time', then continued onwards, until they arrived at a quaint trattoria—little more than a hole in the wall, with a green awning, a narrow door and six small tables set up inside. Each table had a round-based wine bottle with a candle in its top, the legs of wax running down towards the table.

'Gianni, *ciao*,' Luca greeted.

Olivia smiled through the introductions, tried to keep up with the Italian and then took the seat that was offered—affording a beautiful view, not of the beach, but of a small garden at the back of the restaurant, where a single bougainvillea had grown up to form a canopy of explosive purple flowers. Beneath it, there was a pot with a lemon tree, and as she watched a woman walked out, round and dimpled all over, wearing a dark blue apron, and plucked two lemons from the tree. When she turned around and saw Olivia watching, she winked, smiled so dimples dug into her rounded cheeks, then disappeared into a timber door with peeling red paint.

'Oh, Luca.' She turned to look at him, emotions welling in her chest. 'This is all so beautiful.'

He looked around, as though that had never really occurred to him. 'It's very traditional.'

'I love it.'

'I'm glad.'

The waiter appeared with some menus, and Luca explained the dishes to Olivia, translating the words and phrases directly.

'Tortellini—called this because they are like little cakes—torta—filled with cheese and spinach.' He moved his finger down the menu. 'Chicken with lemon and asparagus.'

She selected something light and sat back in her chair, watching him thoughtfully.

'Yes?' He lifted a thick, dark brow, continuing to study her.

Guilt flushed her face. 'What do you mean? I didn't say anything.'

'You have your "question" eyes in.'

'My "question" eyes?'

'How you look at me when something is on your mind. So? Out with it.'

She wanted to laugh, but also nerves were thickening her veins, making it hard to think straight. 'You—'

Gianni reappeared, brandishing two glasses of Prosecco, and two glasses of mineral water.

'Thank you,' she murmured.

When they were alone, Luca continued to stare at her, waiting, one brow cocked.

She flattened her lips. 'You don't have to answer this,' she said gently. 'I know we agreed that neither of us has to share our life story.'

'We did.' He inclined his head in silent agreement of that.

'Only, Pietra mentioned something about Jayne.'

He scowled. 'Did she?'

'Don't be cross with her.'

'I'm not. But I told you she meddles, no?'

'Yes, but only because she loves you so much.'

'And you have a question about my first wife?'

She knew him well enough to know he hated the idea of talking about her, but he stared straight at Olivia, holding her gaze. Fearless. Determined. In control.

'It's not really a question.' She furrowed her brow. 'Only…you must have loved her very much.'

He gripped the stem of his Prosecco flute until his knuckles glowed white. 'Why do you say that?'

'Am I wrong?'

He glared at her, and she knew he wanted to avoid the question, but this was Luca. He didn't shy away from difficult conversations. With a small exhalation of breath, he shifted in his seat, his pose a study in relaxation. Only Olivia could see beyond it, to the tension radiating from his frame.

'I was young and idealistic.'

'So you didn't love her?'

His nostrils flared. 'I would have died for her. I loved her with all that I was, Olivia. But I think, at that age, love felt like a rite of passage. I can't say that I would feel that way for her if we met now.'

Something like danger prickled along Olivia's spine. 'Or for anyone?'

He dipped his head in agreement, without hesitation, and it was that lack of pause that cut her to the quick. If he felt anything for her, she would have seen it then.

'And you believed she loved you?'

Cynicism curled his lips. *'Naturalmente.'* The word dripped with sarcasm. 'It never occurred to me that she was using me for money.'

Indignation flared in Olivia's gut. 'I can't imagine anyone fooling you.'

'I'm not the same man now that I was then.'

'Because of her?'

'Because of life.'

'But Jayne is the reason you've sworn off relationships.'

'I have relationships. You've seen the pictures on the Internet, remember?'

Pain lashed her heart. She forced herself to be brave. 'That's sex. I'm talking about emotion. I'm talking about connection.'

There was a storm raging in his eyes but he didn't look away. 'Sex is the only kind of relationship I'm interested in.'

'Doesn't that get lonely?'

His lips curled into an approximation of a smile, but it spread like ice through her veins. 'Are you lonely, *cara*?'

Beneath the table, his fingers sought her knee first, then higher, to her thigh, shifting the fabric of her skirt with ease so he could touch his skin to hers. She bit back a soft moan.

'What we have is just sex, and yet it suits us both perfectly, no?'

No. She wanted to scream her answer. She wanted to scream it at him as she punched his chest, but how could she? He hadn't said anything wrong. It was perfectly in line with what they'd agreed.

'And after this, you'll find someone else to have "just sex" with?'

It was like laying down a gauntlet, forcing them both to face a reality that Olivia personally wanted to hide from.

Her blood began to hammer inside her, and she could hardly breathe. She waited, and she waited, and agony invaded her every cell, until finally, he shrugged indolently. 'As, I imagine, will you.'

Olivia focused on the view beyond the window, doing everything she could not to react, not to recoil, when the truth was the idea of another man ever making love to her was like setting herself alight. She couldn't fathom it, and she knew, in that moment, that he was wrong. Luca Giovanardi would likely be the only man she ever slept with.

The water rippled against Olivia's breasts, the Lycra of her bathing suit turning an almost copper colour in the pale moonlight. Positano was a patchwork of lights beneath them, the view of the city and, beyond it, the ocean quite mesmerising. Luca came to rest beside her, standing easily against the pool's tiled bottom.

He cast her a smile and the moonlight met his face, bathing it in silver, so he was breathtakingly beautiful. It was an almost perfect moment. Almost, because Olivia couldn't blot out their conversation over lunch. She couldn't ignore the ease with which he faced the prospect of their separation, while she was aware, all the time, of the beating of a drum in the back of her mind, a constant, rhythmic motion, propelling her through time, almost against her will.

In less than a week, she'd leave Italy, and Luca. She had to. It was what they'd agreed. It was what he still wanted. *And what do you want?*

She wanted, with all her heart, to stay. It terrified Olivia to admit that to herself, but she wasn't an idiot. She knew what had been happening the last few weeks. Every look, every touch, every moment they shared had been drumming deep into her soul, making him a part of her in a way she'd sworn she'd never allow any man to be.

That was why she had to leave in a week.

Marriage to a man like Luca was too dangerous. He was too much—too easy to love, and she knew what love did. Her parents had shown her again and again. It was the most powerfully destructive force in the universe, capable of wreaking so much havoc and anger. She'd never allow that to happen to them. It would hurt like hell to leave Luca but at least she could leave while things were still great between them, and carry with her cherished memories of their time together. That was so much better than waiting for their love to turn to hate. She couldn't bear that.

'I came to live with my grandmother, after my divorce. I used to love this view.'

'Used to?'

'Still do,' he murmured, and her heart lurched in her chest.

'What was it like, living here?'

'It was exactly what I needed,' he said, after a beat, and she understood his hesitation—that he was contemplating pushing her to share what was on her mind. She was relieved he didn't.

'In what way?'

'Here, I was able to immerse myself in nature for a time, to strip everything away and focus on simply existing. I would walk to Positano almost every day, take out an old timber boat, catch fish that Pietra and I would eat for lunch, right here on this terrace. I would free dive for scallops, and swim through the caves at the edge of Positano. I walked until my skin burned from the sun, and until my legs were like jelly. I did everything I could to silence my brain, my thoughts, to blot out the real world.'

'What about your friends?'

A snarl curled the corner of his mouth. 'My father's actions affected almost everyone I knew.'

Anger pulsed in her veins. 'So they took it out on you?'

A muscle jerked in his jaw. 'Many lost their fortunes.'

'But you repaid them.'

He lifted his shoulders.

'Your grandmother mentioned one friend who stood by you. I can't remember—'

'Alejandro.'

'You're still friends?'

'More like brothers,' Luca agreed. 'He was the only one. I will always be grateful to him, for standing with me.' He turned away from her, his eyes roaming the horizon. She followed his gaze, the beauty stinging now. It was the last time she'd see it.

'Thank you for bringing me here.' Her voice was hoarse; she cleared her throat. 'I like your grandmother, a lot. I'm sorry I won't get to know her better.'

The air between them grew taut. She heard the unspoken implication of that sentence. The inevitable was coming.

'She would have liked to get to know you, too.'

'When will you tell her about our divorce?'

His features gave nothing away, but he turned towards her slowly, his eyes probing hers, as if to read something in her question, something she couldn't see or say.

'When I have to.'

'You'll continue the charade?'

He frowned. 'It's not exactly a charade.'

'You know what I mean. You'll pretend I'm still here, even when I'm back in England?'

'I simply won't tell her anything at all,' he corrected, then made an effort to soften his words. 'She'll be okay, *cara*. She is used to my short attention span with women.' His smile was barely a flicker of his lips, and the coldness of it turned her core to ice. Not because of Luca, but because of her father, and his supreme control of his emotions, because of the way he could turn on a dime.

He was wrong about Pietra. He clearly didn't

understand how relieved the older woman was that Luca had, apparently, fallen in love. He didn't know what their marriage meant to her. The peace she would get on her deathbed, of believing that he was no longer such a determined loner.

Olivia shivered, despite the balmy warmth of the night. Everything about their surroundings was perfect, but she was cold to the core. 'I think I'll go inside, Luca. I'm tired.'

He watched her swim away, fighting a desire to follow her, to draw her back into the water or to follow her inside. They'd been spending too much time together, despite his best efforts to guard against that. She was putting space between them—and that was wise. The smartest thing to do was to go along with it. After all, in less than a week they'd be living different lives in different countries.

CHAPTER THIRTEEN

As a child, Luca had never counted the sleeps until Christmas, or birthdays, or any life event, and yet he was aware, every minute of the day, of the nights remaining with Olivia, and he resented her that power, he resented their marriage for how easily it had become a part of him. For a man used to living alone, having Olivia at his side was strangely perfect.

Because she was undemanding.

Because she was temporary.

Because there was no risk that she would want more than he could give, that he might come to love her or she might come to love him. The black-and-white agreement they'd made offered protection, and in that protected space he'd come to *enjoy* her company.

His phone began to ring and he glared at it sharply. He wasn't in the mood for interruptions. He ignored it, standing up and striding to his windows, looking down on Rome.

Three more nights. And then what?

And then what? He berated himself angrily. And then, life would continue as it had before. She'd leave, he'd be alone, but he'd be fine— alone was a state he was perfectly used to.

'I've let my assistant know you'll need to use the jet over the weekend.'

Midway through lifting a fork to her mouth, Olivia paused, replacing the bite in her bowl. 'Oh?'

'For your return to the UK. That was the date we agreed, yes?'

Her heart skittered around her chest cavity like an ice skater out of control. She focused on her plate extra hard, staring at the pasta dish until the noodles began to swirl before her eyes. *Don't cry. Don't emote. Don't express anything.* Suddenly she was eight years old again, caught between her father and her mother, in the midst of one of their terrible arguments. She tried to fade into the background then took in a deep breath and pushed a smile to her lips, forcing her eyes to meet his. 'Yes, that's right. But I don't need a jet. I booked a commercial flight ages ago, before we were even married.'

Was she imagining the way he expelled a

rushed breath? Was it a sigh of relief? Or of something else?

'I see.' He took a drink of wine, then replaced the glass quietly on the table. 'You can cancel it.'

Her eyes widened. Hope danced.

'My jet is at your disposal.'

'That's completely unnecessary.'

He shrugged, nonchalant, unconcerned. Her throat felt as though it were lined with acid. 'As you wish.'

I don't wish! She blinked rapidly as she lifted some spaghetti to her mouth, silencing herself before she could make the protestation. This was best—for both of them. It was what they had agreed to, and she needed to go through with it.

Two nights to go. Luca was impatient and unsettled. He couldn't focus. He sat through meeting after meeting, glowering, so his staff assumed a permanently worried air—and he didn't notice. His mind was absorbed by another issue.

Olivia's departure.

A month had seemed like an interminable period of time when they'd first agreed to it. It was longer than he'd spent with any woman, since Jayne. He'd thought it would drag, and that he'd be glad to see her go, but he wasn't an idiot. He couldn't ignore the fact that he was looking forward to her departure in the same way a man might look forward to chopping off his own arm.

So, what to do?

He stood abruptly, and the meeting grew silent. He scanned the room, fixed his glance on his vice president and nodded. 'Take it from here.'

He needed to be alone; he needed to think.

Olivia packed carefully, each item she folded neatly reminding her of their honeymoon, when Luca had surprised her with bag after bag of couture—of a trip she'd had no expectations of, but that had quickly morphed into something way beyond her wildest dreams. In fact, that basically summed up their entire marriage. Nothing was what she'd expected, it had all been so much more.

She heard the closing of the downstairs door and her pulse went into overdrive.

Luca.

She continued folding, one dress after another, her heart stammering in her chest, until she felt him behind her and turned slowly, a practised smile on her face. 'Hello. How was your day?'

She heard the stilted, formal question, so at odds with the relationship they'd developed, and winced.

He stood against the door jamb, casually reclined, as though he had not a care in the world, but there was something in his face, a mask of concentration, that made a mockery of his pose.

'Why are you packing? You don't leave for two nights.'

Two days. The words were like thunderclaps in her chest.

'I like to be organized,' she offered with a tight smile.

He said nothing for some time, simply watched her, and then, finally, his words broke the silence that was tightening the air in the room.

'I've been thinking.'

She continued with what she was doing, but her actions were stilted, because she was having to concentrate hard on such a simple task. Everything felt unnatural.

'Well, that's good, I suppose.' She aimed for levity, even when her cells were reverberating with a desperate need to know *what* he'd been thinking.

'When we agreed to get married, it was for a very specific purpose. Each of us benefited, and we made sure the marriage would work for us both—by having clear-cut rules in place.'

She arched a brow, her smile a quirk of her lips. 'I remember.' She cleared her throat, reaching for another dress. He pushed up off the door jamb, coming into the room, hands in pockets.

'When we agreed to sleep together, it was the same thing—we made an arrangement, we drew out the terms of what we were doing, to make sure we were on the same page.'

She nodded once, placing the dress in her suitcase, her fingers shaking a little.

'One of the terms was that our marriage would end after a month.'

She reached for a blouse. 'I'm familiar with what we agreed.' Her response was sharper than she'd intended.

His eyes narrowed. 'And what if we were to renegotiate the terms of our marriage?'

Her heart leaped without her consent. 'Which terms, in particular?'

'The term in which you leave.'

The world stopped spinning. She stared at Luca, trying not to react, trying not to feel, but her heart was exploding with something terrifyingly like joy.

'Hear me out.' He lifted a hand placatingly,

perhaps misreading her expression. 'This marriage is obviously different—better—than either of us thought it would be. Why walk away from it after only a month?'

Her breath burned in her lungs.

'Why stay?' she asked instead, because she knew the answer she would give, but what was Luca's? Everything hung on his response. She stood there, waiting, and hating, because in that moment she became a child again, waiting for approval, waiting for more than it was possible to be given—by the man in front of her, at least. But Luca wasn't her father. What if she was wrong? What if?

'Because this works,' he said quickly, with no idea of how those words fell like the executioner's blade. 'We're good together, and a marriage like this—a marriage that's logical and sensible—suits us both.'

She bit down on her lower lip, rather than contradicting him.

'You saw your parents' disastrous marriage and swore it would never be for you. But what I'm offering is so different. I'm not suggesting we stay married because we're in love, nor because we're emotionally involved. I'm suggesting it because we're neither of those things. I like being around you, I like spending time together, I love sleeping with you. We make a good team. Isn't that worth staying for? Worth fighting for?'

Her heart was racing far too fast. A thousand things flashed into her mind, but she wasn't sure if she was brave enough to say them. He talked about fighting for their marriage, but she couldn't. She couldn't fight for what she'd never get—her mother had spent a lifetime doing that, fighting for the love of her husband, and it was withheld, cruelly, callously. Luca wouldn't ever intentionally hurt Olivia, but the effect would be the same regardless, because he'd never love her.

She stood straighter as the thought struck her like a lightning bolt, acceptance right behind. Of course, she loved him. The thought sank her like a lead balloon. She *loved* him. She loved her husband. Her eyes were as wide as saucers as she looked at him, shock reverberating through her.

'I know your experience with marriage was traumatic. The way your parents were with each other, the way your father treated your mother.' He moved closer to her and she flinched, because her heart was too raw for him to touch her. 'The love they shared turned to hate.' He lifted a hand to her cheek and her eyes swept shut, the contact sending shock waves through her body. 'That would never happen with us. A marriage that's built on respect and friendship, a partnership rather than a romance, protects us both.'

'But can't you hear how cold it is?'

His eyes flared. 'There is *nothing* cold between us.'

She bit down on her lip. 'I don't mean sex. I mean—emotionally. I don't want what you're describing.'

His eyes darkened. 'You don't want more of what we've shared this last month?'

Of course she did. She yearned for that.

'You don't want to depend on anyone,' he said gently. 'You want independence, at all costs. I'm not asking you to sacrifice that. I'm not asking you to share more of yourself than you're willing to share. That's why this works so well. Without love, we can be calm and dispassionate, we can meet each other's needs, we can be friends who see the world together, who live side by side. Hell, we can even share a family of our own one day, without any risk of getting hurt. Can't you see how right that is?'

No, it was all wrong. So much of what he was

offering made her heart swell, because it was what she wanted—to see the world with him, to have a family with him, but without love? Even when she had seen the dark side of love, and was terrified by its power, she knew she couldn't stay with Luca, loving him as she did. It was better to leave, to nurse a broken heart, than to stay and yearn for what he'd never give.

'It's not what I want,' she whispered gently.

So gently he had to lean closer to hear her words properly.

'I have a life back in England, Luca.'

'Do you? Because it never sounds like much of a life, when you talk about it.'

Her eyes dipped between them. He was right; he knew her too well. She swallowed past a lump in her throat, and then his finger was lifting her chin, tilting her face to his.

'I have responsibilities.'

'So we'll go back for the weekend,' he said with a nonchalant shrug. 'It's a couple of hours in a plane.'

'No.' Now that she understood her feelings, she couldn't pretend any longer. The time they had left was going to be a minefield. She fidgeted her hands in front of her, then lifted one to his chest. 'We had a deal.'

Disbelief was etched in the lines of his face. 'And that deal originally included no sex. Then we realised we were attracted to one another and we changed the deal. Why can't we do that again?'

She dipped her head forward.

'Try it for three months. If this isn't working, we can both walk away then.'

But she wouldn't be able to walk away. If she was already finding the prospect to be a form of torture, how hard would it be in twelve weeks' time?

'I don't want to change our agreement.'

Something shifted in his features. Rejection? Her heart ached. She was hurting him. And he was hurting her. It was exactly what they'd sworn they wouldn't do.

'I see.'

'No, you don't,' she said with a small shake of her head.

He lifted a finger to her lips, silencing her. 'It's okay. It was just an idea, *cara*.'

She opened her mouth to explain, then slammed it shut. Just an idea. No big deal. He didn't care. It didn't matter. None of this did. When she left he'd replace her because, ultimately, she meant nothing to him. She was a convenient wife, just as she'd always been a convenient daughter, flying beneath the radar. Olivia's heart was on the line, Luca was simply trying to manoeuvre a beneficial relationship into lasting a bit longer. She'd said 'no', and now he was brushing it aside. 'Shall we eat out?'

She barely slept. Their strange conversation played over and over in her mind, tormenting her, making her doubt the wisdom of her response, so she wondered why she hadn't just accepted his suggestion. It would mean more time with him. Wasn't that what she wanted?

But at what cost?

Dawn light filtered into his room and, beside her, Luca woke, pushing out of bed and striding into the en suite bathroom. Olivia rolled over and pretended to sleep, pretended not to care that it was the first morning in weeks they hadn't made love. Her heart was splintering into a thousand little shards.

The house felt like a mausoleum suddenly. Olivia couldn't find peace, couldn't get comfortable. She didn't want to go out—she was too tired from a sleepless night—and she was finished packing. There was nothing left to occupy her, which left her mind with too much time to fret, to obsess, to panic.

Olivia caught a reflection of herself as she moved from one room to the next and stopped in her tracks. Her face was drawn, her lips turned downwards, her eyes dull, devoid of spark. She looked like her mother often had. Miserable.

Was this what heartache felt like? How had her mother lived with it for so many years?

And suddenly, Olivia knew she couldn't stay any longer. One more night sounded simple enough, but it would be a torment beyond what she could manage. She was turning into her mother, allowing herself to be hurt, and Olivia knew one thing: she wanted better than that. She pulled her phone from her back pocket and began arranging the logistics, bringing her flight forward and booking a car.

It felt surreal to coordinate this, and wrong to do so without Luca's knowledge, but wasn't her independence something she valued? They were two strangers, really, regardless of what had happened in the last month. She'd fought hard—not for their marriage in the end, but for her own life, for her independence—and now she could step into it and enjoy the fruits of her labour. She could go home and see Sisi, and know that her sister would never have to make the kind of pragmatic marriage Olivia had.

She told herself it was relief she was experiencing as the cab driver loaded her suitcase into the boot, the engine idling. She gave one last look at his exquisite home, then slid into the back seat of the car, dark glasses in place.

It was only once she'd checked in her suitcase at the buzzing Fiumicino airport that she dared to call Luca. She'd contemplated leaving a note at his house, but that had felt wrong. And she'd known she couldn't see him again, couldn't say what she needed to say face to face. It was cowardly, but self-preservation instincts were in overdrive.

He answered after one ring. 'Olivia.'

God, she would miss hearing him say her name. 'Luca.'

'How are you?'

She squeezed her eyes shut as tears filled her gaze. 'I'm fine,' she lied, shaking her head a little. 'Look, there was so much I didn't say last night, because I couldn't find the words at the time, and I was scared to admit what I wanted, when you were offering something so reasonable and sensible, something I might have jumped at, in another life.'

Each of his breaths was audible as he waited for her to continue.

'The thing is, the way my father treated my mother, it's just like you said—love turned to hate. They did love each other at one time, and they were happy, and then things went wrong, he never forgave her, and she was miserable. She's still miserable. There's nothing quite so awful as being married to someone you love, who doesn't love you back.' The words hung between them like little blades.

'But what I was offering cut that concern out of the equation.'

Her smile was bitter. 'For you, perhaps, but not for me.'

'I don't understand.'

'I know that.' Despite her efforts, a sob caught in her throat, punctuating the final word.

'Olivia, what is it? You're upset.'

'No.' She blinked around the terminal, the fluorescent light too bright, even with her dark sunglasses. A voice came over the speakers, muffled by static. She stood, pulling her handbag strap over her shoulder.

'Where are you?'

'I'm at the airport.' She sniffed.

'The airport? What the hell? Your flight's tomorrow.'

'I moved it forward.'

'Why?'

'What's the point in drawing this out? We want different things.'

'Because I asked you to stay another three months?'

'Because you asked me to stay *only* another three months.'

'To begin with,' he insisted, muffled noise in the background. 'You were the one who balked at the idea of a real marriage—'

'But that's not what you were offering.'

'You know what I mean—a lasting marriage, like we have now, but ongoing. I thought three months would reassure you that there was an escape clause.'

'I don't want an escape clause.'

'Then why are you at the airport?'

She groaned, tilting her head back to stare at the ceiling. 'I realised something, last night. When you were offering a perfectly reasonable loveless relationship, a marriage founded, in fact, on the absence of love, I came to understand that it's the exact opposite of what I want.

I love you, Luca. Somehow, I fell in love with you, despite having sworn I'd never love anyone. And if I stay here in Rome, with you, I'll start to hope you'll love me back, and the hoping will make me miserable, just like my mother was.'

'What did you just say?'

She moved towards the boarding gate, tears streaming down her cheeks now.

'My worst fear is being married to someone I love, who doesn't love me back. I know what that can do to a person, and I can't do it to my-self—even for one more night. Now that I un-derstand how I feel about you, I have no choice but to leave.'

'Olivia—'

'It's okay,' she interrupted. 'I've thought about this from every angle. I just wish I was brave enough to have said this to your face, so that you could see the genuine gratitude in my eyes when I thank you for what you did for me.'

He groaned almost inaudibly. 'Stay. Spend to-night with me.' His voice was deep and throaty. 'Come home.'

'But this isn't my home,' she said with final-ity. 'And you're not really my husband. You never were. A marriage isn't a marriage without love, we both know that.' She waited for him to disagree, bracing for it, and then, after a long pause, shook her head. 'Goodbye, Luca.'

CHAPTER FOURTEEN

'OH, COME ON,' she groaned, slapping her forehead as the announcement came over the PA.

'Owing to a technical issue with the landing wheel, Aster Airline flight 251 to London Heathrow has been delayed. We apologise for the inconvenience. Another update will be provided in thirty minutes. Thank you for your patience.'

Olivia ground her teeth together, scanning the departures board, hoping a different airline might be making the same trip to London, so she could book another seat, but there were no other flights for the next two hours.

Resigning herself to her fate, she strode towards the newsagent's, browsing magazines, looking for something, anything, to distract herself with. But a sense of claustrophobia was clawing at her. Having decided she wanted to leave Rome, that she needed to leave Rome, she found the delay completely unacceptable.

She chose two magazines at random, paid for them without looking at the covers, then found a seat apart from most of the crowd. Rather than reading the magazines, she stared out of the large, heavily tinted windows, at the concourse, watching as passengers disembarked planes directly onto the runway, from skinny staircases, walking in organised lines towards the building. Planes took off, others landed, but after thirty minutes another announcement was made: their plane would be delayed at least another hour.

It was tempting to go to the information desk and ask for more information, but the queue snaked halfway through their seating area, and the staff member there was already looking harried and stressed. Olivia had no interest in adding to her load.

She continued to watch the happenings of the airport, the piercing blue of Rome's sky making a mockery of her mood.

In her peripheral vision, she was aware of another traveller approaching and she bristled, wanting company like she wanted a hole in the head. She kept her gaze resolutely focused on the window, staring at the sky, actively discouraging any attempt at communication.

'Do you need a lift, *cara*?'

Her heart went into overdrive and her head turned towards him in complete shock, his voice jolting something inside her to life. She was too overcome to pretend calm. How grateful she was that her dark glasses were still in place!

'Luca! What are you doing here?'

'Did you think I would not move heaven and earth to finish our conversation?'

She stood up to meet his eyes, not liking the height disadvantage of her seated position.

'We did finish our conversation.'

'Too abruptly.'

'What else is there to say?'

He looked around, and in that moment she allowed herself the brief weakness of drinking him in, all suit-clad, six and a half feet of him. The power of his physique took her breath away, as it almost always did.

'More than I'd care to discuss here,' he said with a shake of his head, holding out his hand. 'Come with me.'

She looked at his hand as though it were a bundle of snakes.

'My jet is fuelled up. I'll fly you to London. We can speak on the way.'

Her lips parted. The offer of the flight was

tempting—but to have her escape route shared with the very man she was running away from?

His eyes darkened as her hesitation became obvious.

'Fine,' he ground out. 'You can take the flight without me.' He lifted one finger to the air. 'On one condition.'

'Another deal?'

'Yes.'

'What is it?'

'Give me ten minutes first. To talk. Privately.'

Privately. A shiver ran down her spine, desire sparking in her belly. She looked away. 'Okay, that's fair enough.' Had she really thought she could avoid this? 'Where?'

But he took her hand, drawing her with him, away from the crowds, the disgruntled voices, and right back out of the terminal, towards a central concourse, and then across it. Neither of them spoke—not even when he gestured for her to enter a set of timber doors ahead of him.

A first-class lounge, so exclusive it wasn't even badged, awaited them. Luca was clearly known here by name. Here, it was easy to find a private corner—there were only half a dozen or so other travellers, and the room was enormous.

At a table in the distant corner, he pulled out

a seat. She eyed it sceptically, nervously, then eased herself into it.

'Thank you.'

He took the seat opposite, and the table seemed to shrink about three sizes. She toyed with her hands in her lap, then forced herself to stop, to meet his gaze. To be strong enough to do this.

'What would you like to discuss?'

His laugh was a short, sharp sound, totally lacking amusement. 'What you said on the phone, for one.'

'Which part?'

His eyes narrowed. 'Which part do you think?'

She compressed her lips, the answer obvious. 'Why?'

'Olivia, you told me you *never* wanted to fall in love. When we agreed to this marriage—'

'I know that. I'm sorry.'

'You're sorry?'

'We had a deal. I broke it. I never meant to. I didn't *want* to love you.'

'How do you know it's love?'

She frowned, the question totally surprising her. 'How do I know the sky is blue or the earth is round?'

'Science?'

She smiled despite the heaviness in her heart.

'Fact. And this is fact. Not scientific, perhaps, but no less real.'

'Since when?'

Another question she hadn't expected. 'I can't say. Probably the moment you heard me out. I half expected you to get me thrown out of that party in Rome. That you didn't, that you listened and agreed to my crazy proposal, showed me what a decent guy you were. And every day since—'

'And every night?'

'Yes, every night.' She swallowed. 'But this isn't just about sex. I mean, that's a part of what I love, but it's so much more than that.'

He stood up, scraping his chair backwards, pacing towards the windows, gazing for a moment at the aeroplanes lined up on the tarmac, their tails forming a perfect line, then turning, staring at her as if pulling her apart piece by piece. 'The thing is, Olivia, I need to know that you know, beyond a shadow of a doubt. Because I thought I was in love, once, and I believed my wife loved me, but it was the worst mistake of my life. And yet, the impact of Jayne's breaking up with me is nothing compared to this.' He returned to the table, bracing his palms on the edge. 'With her, my pride was hurt. I was blind-sided. But losing you—'

She held her breath, her features contorted by confusion.

'I can't have you say that you love me, if you are then going to decide you don't. I can't let this be a real marriage, in every way, unless you promise me that's what you want. Don't you see, Olivia? I suggested a continuation of what we had because it was safe. What you're offering, what you're asking for, is filled with risks.'

'Yes.' She nodded, her heart soaring at what he was unintentionally revealing. Or was he? Her own feelings burned so brightly, she feared she'd lost the ability to comprehend his. 'I'm aware of that. Like the risk that you might not love me back. Or that your love for me might turn to hate, just as my father's did for my mother.'

'I know enough about love turning to hate. I had a masterclass in it with Jayne. But that doesn't mean I would ever hurt you. Not like your father hurt your mother.' His eyes probed hers. 'Ask yourself if I could ever be capable of the things he did, or if you could ever act as Jayne did. You know the answer to that.'

She bit back a sob.

'I love you because you're nothing like him,'

she whispered, dipping her head forward. 'But that doesn't mean you won't hurt me. That you're not hurting me now.'

He crouched down in front of her face, reaching out and removing her glasses, placing them on the table softly. At the sight of her tear-reddened eyes, he cursed softly. 'I don't want you to go.'

'I know that.' Anguish tore through her. 'But I can't stay.'

'Even for love?'

'My loving you isn't enough. You know that.'

'What about the fact I love you, too? What about the fact I am terrified of what that means, but I'm here, saying it anyway, because I know one thing for certain—if I lose you, I will regret it for the rest of my life.'

Her lips parted in surprise.

He lifted up, curling a hand around her cheek. 'I didn't realise, until you called me an hour ago, and told me you loved me, that the reason I can't bear the thought of you leaving our marriage as agreed is because I don't want you to leave—ever.'

'You said that last night,' she groaned. 'But it's not enough to want me to stay. That's *not* love, it's convenience.'

He pressed a finger to her lips. 'I asked you to stay, not because I want to continue our convenient arrangement, but because I don't want to live without you. Because you have given meaning to my life, because you have made me smile again, *cara*, and because with you, not only do I feel complete, I *feel*, in here, after years of nothing.' He tapped a hand to his heart. 'Is there any part of you that wants to walk away from this?'

She squeezed her eyes shut, everything she'd ever known to be true in her life like an enormous impediment. 'No,' she whispered, finally. 'But I'm scared.'

'And I am terrified,' he countered. 'I thought I had been through the pits of hell when Jayne left me. I thought that was as bad as it got. But now, I imagine a life without you, I imagine you waking up and deciding you no longer want me in your life, and I know that it would be ten thousand times worse.'

She blinked, his passion obvious.

'Yet, I am kneeling here now, asking you to stay with me regardless because, whatever I fear, a life with you is worth the risk.'

Her throat was too thick with unshed tears for Olivia to speak coherently. A muffled sob escaped.

'I do not want you simply to stay,' he said, after a moment. 'I want you to marry me, for real. This time, in front of family, friends, the world. I want everyone to join in the celebration of our love, to witness our commitment, to understand that I am pledging myself to you, for the rest of my life. Love is a leap of faith, but what is the alternative, Olivia? To both run from our past, to keep ourselves closed off?' He lifted closer to her, so their mouths were separated by only an inch. 'To lose one another? This? For me to live each day without you, without what we share? Is there anything worse than that?'

Anguish tortured her, but it was pierced by hope and joy. She shook her head, tears rolling down her cheeks. 'There is nothing worse than losing you,' she confirmed.

'And so you never shall,' he promised. 'Olivia, the last time we discussed marrying, it was with very carefully worded conditions in place. Now, I ask you this: Will you marry me? With no condition, no caution, no limitation on our joy, our future? Marry me, stand beside me—your own person, as independent as you seek to be—but with my companionship, my love, and always, always, my support.'

A smile cracked her face. She closed the rest of the distance between them, kissing him, and into the kiss, into his soul, she said the word 'yes', over and over and over again, because she felt it in every fibre of her being, every part of her own soul. She loved him, and always would. While it was true that love was a gamble, a leap of faith, the strength of their love had given them both wings to catch them, should they fall. She trusted Luca, and knew her heart to be safe with him—there was nothing she wanted more than to return to their life, as his wife, and to truly start living.

'Luca?'

'Mmm?'

'Let's go home.'

His eyes widened, the meaning of her statement not lost on him.

'*Sì, cara.* Let's go home.'

Luca loved his wife, and he loved her in a way that had expanded his soul, had expanded everything he knew about life. He'd learned that the fear he'd felt was actually excitement, that stepping into a life with Olivia gave him an adrenaline rush every day. A month after their airport reunion, they were married, and only one week later Olivia realised the reason for her changeable appetite and sudden aversion to cured meats and alcohol. A honeymoon baby, or close to, conceived during their first week together in Rome, when they had been making love and falling in love all at the same time. So that now, eight months after Olivia had told Luca she loved him, and he'd realised how he felt about her, he stared down at a little infant wrapped in pink, a new kind of love stealing through him, happiness making him feel as though he could take on the world.

'She is perfect, *cara*. How clever you are.'

'I think we can both take credit for her,' Olivia said with a smile, head pressed back against the crisp white hospital pillow. Luca had never loved her more.

'That is very kind of you.'

'Would you hand her to me?' Olivia asked, tired, but arms aching to once again hold their hours-old daughter.

'Certo.' He picked up their newborn, cradling her to his chest a moment before snuggling her into Olivia's arms, and watching as their baby nestled against her. Completion wrapped around him. Everything in his life was perfect.

* * *

The sound of wheels on linoleum woke Olivia, and a moment later Luca appeared, pushing Pietra into the hospital room. Three days after giving birth, and Olivia was feeling somewhat normal, except for breasts that suddenly felt so enormous she wasn't sure how she could stand without toppling over.

'Ah, Nonna.' Olivia smiled, pushing up to standing and wincing slightly.

'Stay, stay,' Pietra insisted, so much frailer than the last time they'd seen each other, but with eyes still sparkling with intelligence and wit, and a ready smile softening her slender face. Her continued wellness was, doctors kept saying, a 'miracle', but Olivia knew better. Pietra wasn't finished yet—from the moment she'd learned of Olivia's pregnancy, it had seemed to give her a new lease on life, a determination to stave off the ravages of her disease, or perhaps it was fate, being as kind to Pietra as it had been to Luca and Olivia, when it had delivered them into one another's arms. 'You do not need to get up.'

'I want to bring the baby to you,' Olivia demurred, love in her eyes as they met Luca's.

'Thank you,' he mouthed.

She moved to the plastic-sided crib and removed the swaddle, then lifted her daughter out. She placed her carefully in Pietra's arms, aware that Luca was there, waiting, ready to intervene if Pietra's strength failed her.

'She is so lovely.' A tear slid down Pietra's cheek. 'So much like you, Olivia.'

Olivia stroked their baby's head. 'I see a fair bit of Giovanardi in her as well.'

'Do you?' Pride touched Pietra's face.

'Oh, yes. She has your eyes.'

The baby grabbed Pietra's finger, curling her tiny fingers around its frail length.

'Does she have a name yet?'

'Actually, that is something we wanted to discuss with you,' Luca said, nodding, gently prompting Olivia to continue.

'We were wondering how you would feel about us calling her Pietra.'

Pietra's lips parted in surprise. 'I would be touched, of course. Are you sure?'

'It's the only name we considered,' Olivia promised. 'To us, she's already Pietra.'

'Luca, look!'

'What is it, *cara*?' On the eve of their tenth wedding anniversary, Luca emerged from the kitchen, apron tied around his waist, looking impossibly sexy. She loved him in myriad ways, but his determination to learn to cook for her and their children, and to be a present, hands-on father and husband, made her fall in love with him more and more each day.

'Look what I found!' She carried the item, wrapped carefully in bubble wrap, to Luca, triumph in her features.

'A toy? I don't know. What is it? The children's teeth?'

Olivia laughed, lifting a finger to her lips. 'You know the *fatina dei denti* takes those away.' She held the bubble wrap out to him. 'I was looking for my wedding dress, on a whim. Pietra was asking about it.'

'I am not surprised it was our daughter, rather than the twins.' He laughed with paternal indulgence.

'Rafaello and Fiero are busy with their soccer match, of course.' She rolled her eyes, because it seemed to be all their seven-year-old sons cared for at present. 'Anyway, I was looking in the box of wedding things, and found this.'

He peeled the tab of the sticky tape, casting his wife a rueful glance as she hopped from foot to foot, until eventually he revealed what was within: the Murano *fenice*. He looked from the bird to Olivia, shaking his head. 'I had quite forgotten about this.'

'Yes, me too. It's exquisite. Do you remember the day we chose him?'

'I do.'

'How did we ever forget?'

'Life,' he said with a warm smile. 'We have been busy living.'

Happiness spread through Olivia. 'Well, now I don't feel quite so bad. Where shall we put it?'

'Somewhere prominent,' Luca said, and then, as an afterthought, 'But far from the boys' football kicks.'

She laughed, sashaying through the living room, placing the bird atop the grand piano little Pietra was obsessed with playing each night.

'Perfect. And here it will stand to remind us that, from the ashes, good things really can rise,' Luca murmured, wrapping his arms around his wife, pressing his chin to her shoulder. They stared at the bird, content, and grateful, all at once.

'What time is Sienna arriving?'

Olivia glanced at her wristwatch. 'Their flight should land any minute.'

'Then I had better get back to the kitchen.' He

kissed her cheek, then spun her in the circle of his arms, seeking her lips, never able to pass up an opportunity to taste his beloved wife.

'Are you sure you don't have any spare time?' she asked silkily, wrapping her arms behind his back, just as the twins burst into the room, speaking in rapid-fire Italian about alleged on-field grievances, so Olivia and Luca shared a glance of amusement and pulled slightly apart.

'Come into the kitchen and tell me about it, *terramotti*,' Luca said, then, leaning closer and whispering, purely for Olivia's benefit, 'Tonight, *mi amore*. Tonight.'

It was a promise he intended to keep—for that night, and every night for the rest of their lives.

* * * * *

LET'S TALK
Romance

For exclusive extracts, competitions
and special offers, find us online:

f facebook.com/millsandboon

⊙ @millsandboonuk

𝕏 @millsandboon

Or get in touch on 0844 844 1351*

For all the latest titles coming soon,
visit millsandboon.co.uk/nextmonth

*Calls cost 7p per minute plus your phone company's price per
minute access charge